DYING TO DECORATE

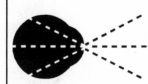

This Large Print Book carries the
Seal of Approval of N.A.V.H.

DYING TO DECORATE

CYNDY SALZMANN

THORNDIKE PRESS
A part of Gale, Cengage Learning

GALE
CENGAGE Learning

Detroit • New York • San Francisco • New Haven, Conn • Waterville, Maine • London

GALE
CENGAGE Learning·

Thorndike Press® Large Print Christian Mystery.
The text of this Large Print edition is unabridged.
Other aspects of the book may vary from the original edition.
Set in 16 pt. Plantin.
Printed on permanent paper.

LIBRARY OF CONGRESS CATALOGING-IN-PUBLICATION DATA

Salzmann, Cynthia S.
   Dying to decorate : a Friday Afternoon Club mystery / by Cyndy Salzmann.
     p. cm. — (Thorndike Press large print Christian mystery)
     ISBN-13: 978-1-4104-1111-2 (alk. paper)
     ISBN-10: 1-4104-1111-7 (alk. paper)
     1. Women detectives—Fiction. 2. Female friendship—Fiction. 3. Housewives—Fiction. 4. Large type books. I. Title.
     PS3619.A446D95 2008
     813'.6—dc22   2008034275

Published in 2008 by arrangement with Howard Books, a division of Simon & Schuster, Inc.

Printed in Mexico
2 3 4 5 6 7 12 11 10 09 08

To Mary, Liz, Shirley, P.J., Mirm, Jean, Danette, Lorna, Deb, and Denise

ACKNOWLEDGMENTS

I am indebted to many people who helped make this book a reality.

Philis Boultinghouse and Chrys Howard of Howard Publishing Company, for taking a chance on a new novelist. Without their encouragement and persistence, this book would still be an idea — and I would still be behind on laundry.

Ramona Cramer Tucker, for her excellent editing and sweet encouragement. What a privilege it has been to partner with you on this project!

Susan Sleeman, my critique partner, for her help in focusing the story during a very busy time.

The research staff of the Stuhr Museum of the Prairie Pioneer in Grand Island, Nebraska, for providing invaluable historical data from their archives, as well as the opportunity to see history come to life through their many exhibits.

Historian Wanda Ewalt of Tabor, Iowa, who graciously gave me a private tour of the Todd House, the home of a Congregationalist minister, used as a station on the Underground Railroad.

Staff and resources of the Omaha Public Library for research assistance — again and again.

My coffee-shop pals, Ricci and Liz, who kept my cup filled at my "satellite" office.

My supportive in-laws, Don and Lois Salzmann, who gave me use of their delightful carriage house while I finished the manuscript. A writer's dream . . .

Amanda Warden, Forensic Scientist, for sharing her expertise in the area of serology.

My mother and stepfather, Betty and Clarence Contestabile, for sharing fabulous recipes and colorful Italian heritage.

My sweet and patient children, Freddy, Liz, and Anna, who pitched in on household chores to help me meet my deadline.

My dear, dear husband, John, for his support and encouragement — and help with the laundry. I love you, sweetheart!

And, of course, my own Friday Afternoon Club — Mary, Liz, Shirley, P.J., Mirm, Jean, Danette, Lorna, Deb, and Denise — for your treasured friendship. You will always be close to my heart!

8

Finally, but most importantly, Almighty God, for allowing me to serve Him with my writing.

Let the favor of the Lord our God be
upon us;
And confirm for us the work of our
hands.

PSALM 90:17

■ ■ ■ ■

CHAPTER ONE

■ ■ ■ ■

I'm-So-Sorry Snickerdoodles

1 cup butter, room temperature
1 1/2 cups sugar
2 eggs
2 3/4 cups flour
3 teaspoons baking powder
1/2 teaspoon salt
1/2 cup sugar
1/2 teaspoon cinnamon

Instructions

1. In a bowl, cream together butter, sugar, and eggs.
2. In a separate bowl, mix together flour, baking powder, and salt. Add gradually to creamed mixture.
3. Chill dough for one hour. Shape into balls the size of walnuts.
4. Roll balls into mixture of 1/2 cup sugar and 1/2 teaspoon cinnamon.

Place on cookie sheet.

5. Bake at 400 degrees until slightly brown — about eight minutes.
6. Remove from pan to cool on rack. Makes about 4 dozen cookies.

DOUBLE MOCHA FRAPPUCCINO

1 cup double-strength coffee, cold
1/2 cup milk
1/4 cup half-and-half
1/4 cup chocolate sauce
2 large scoops vanilla ice cream
3 tablespoons sugar
1 cup ice

Instructions

1. Mix all ingredients in blender for 10 seconds on low, then 20 seconds on high.
2. Serve with whipped cream and chocolate shavings on top, if desired.

"Yes!" Islam the phone back in its cradle, sending the dog skittering across the kitchen floor. "Don't worry, Daisy. You're not in trouble — this time! But don't think I don't know about your midnight raids in the kitchen trash. What do you think gives you the kind of gas that clears a room? I'm onto you, puppy dog, and it's only a matter of time before I catch you in the act!"

Great. Here I am, a grown woman, talking to a dog about gas. Next I'll be expecting Daisy to pull a pack of Tums from her collar. I am so ready for FAC!

Before you get the wrong idea about my sanity — or lack of it — let me introduce myself. My name is Elizabeth Harris. Liz, to most. In addition to Daisy, our precocious Westie, I share our home in Omaha, Nebraska, with a very patient husband, two teenagers, and a "tween." Once a week I write a lifestyle column for our local newspaper — even though these days my life seems to lack a significant amount of style. Let's face it. How stylish can a woman actually feel climbing out of a minivan?

It's so interesting to look back at the glamorous dreams of youth. In high school my goal was to get my hair to look like Farrah Fawcett's — a glamorous crime-fighter on the TV show *Charlie's Angels*. But instead of gently waving tresses, all I could produce after a frustrating session with my curling iron were two tight curls that resembled skinny sausages framing my face. In college I decided to cut my long hair and pursue a career as a newswoman like Mary Tyler Moore.

After graduating from journalism school, I landed a job as a cub reporter at the local TV station. The glamour of this profession began to wear off shortly after our first child arrived. Returning to work after maternity leave, I was determined to "have it all" — great career, fabulous marriage, wonderful family. Not even willing to give up nursing, I dutifully pumped my milk in the ladies' rest room at the station twice a day. After a long night of reporting election returns, I discovered that trying to "have it all" carries a price I wasn't sure I wanted to pay . . .

"Liz, they want to go live in two minutes," said my photographer, Andy. "Are you ready for your stand-up?"

"Sure," I replied, adjusting my earpiece. "Does Eric have my leadin?"

"I'll check."

I composed my thoughts while Andy communicated with the station. Smoothing my hair and straightening my blouse, I suddenly felt that familiar tingling known only to nursing mothers.

No, not now. Please not now.

"OK, Liz," said Andy, holding up his fingers, "in three, two . . ." He pointed his finger at me as the little red light of the camera went on, indicating we were on the air.

I pasted a smile on my face and attempted to listen to the anchor's question. But all I could think about was that my milk had begun to let down. On television. Live.

I knew what I needed to do to stop the inevitable flow. Put firm pressure on my breasts. Unfortunately, my training from the La Leche League didn't cover how to gracefully do this when in front of a live television audience.

The anchor's voice interrupted my panic. "It looks like there's a lot of celebrating down there, Liz. I assume they are pretty happy with the returns."

Instinct kicked in as I finished my report, including an uncomfortable interview with the campaign manager, who seemed intent on staring over my shoulder. When the red light on the camera finally clicked off, Andy sheepishly pointed out the reason for the man's unusual behavior: two wet ovals decorated my blouse. I did the next report

17

in my overcoat and turned in my resignation the next morning . . .

But back to the question of maintaining sanity as a stay-at-home mom. Believe it or not, I *am* able to make it through most days without trying to coax a verbal response from the family dog. However, to be brutally honest, a regular dose of what I've fondly come to call FAC is crucial to helping me walk the narrow path of pleasant wife and mother without falling into the abyss and emerging as "the hateful hag."

Although the hateful hag cleverly hides from the outside world, all mothers know how she strains to break her carefully woven leash. For some of us, the hag may rear her loathsome head while trying to arbitrate a battle between siblings over a toy, computer time, or — in the case of teenagers — the car keys. As outlined in our parenting classes, we have taken several cleansing breaths in an effort to keep our composure. But before we know it, the leash snaps! We find ourselves with hands clamped tightly over our ears, shrieking, "Stop it! Stop it! Stop it! Stop it! Stop it!"

Not a pretty picture . . . and certainly one not covered in the Positive Parenting curriculum.

For other moms, the hateful hag may show up in response to what her family considers a simple question, such as, "What's for dinner?" Unfortunately, family members have asked the mother in this situation this same question *every night* for the last fourteen years. Without even realizing hag has slipped out, this characteristically pleasant mother whirls around with a wild look in her eyes and responds with something like, "Why are you asking ME what's for dinner? Do I look like I know what's for dinner? Am I a walking menu? Do I have pots hanging from my belt? A roast around my neck?" Stunned family members slink from the room, whispering among themselves that it might be a good night to pick up pizza.

Although we hate to admit it — often denying the fact to our graves — every mother struggles to keep her hag in check. But when that wicked witch does break free, even for a few moments, we quickly regret our tirades and assuage our guilt by spending hours baking "make-up" cookies or doing chores previously assigned to the kids. FAC is my secret weapon against the hateful hag.

Have I piqued your interest yet? Are you wondering what in the world those magic letters *FAC* represent? Could it be a secret elixir? Some new form of therapy? Perhaps a relaxing spa treatment? Better yet, a box of decadent dark chocolates with macadamia nuts?

Not quite. FAC — short for Friday Afternoon Club — is a group of women (Lucy, Jessie, Marina, Mary Alice, Kelly, and me) who get together on Friday afternoons for that vital shot of "girl time" that all women need but too often sacrifice. There's no agenda. No projects. No menu. Just a couple of hours to relax, recharge, and reconnect at the end of a long week.

At one time we tried to come up with a clever name for the group. But because the demands of our small children left us little energy for creativity, we stuck with FAC. As the years have gone by, we've noticed the name has a definite advantage. Think about it. We *never* have to ask when our little group is getting together. The meeting time is contained in the name. My mother tells me I won't truly appreciate this stroke of genius until menopause.

FAC began about ten years ago as a way to help moms in our neighborhood remember that there are people who are interested in what we have to say — aside from what's for dinner, the location of a sippy cup, if a soccer uniform is clean, and most importantly, why our tomatoes can't talk like the one on the VeggieTales DVD. Not that these aren't pressing questions. It's just nice to have a little variety.

Today our group is much more than a source for adult conversation. We "get" each other the way only other women can. In spite of the arguments of radical feminism, the female species is very different from the male. We are extremely relational and nurture this need through communication . . . *lots* of communication. In fact, we can easily wear our spouses out with the desire to — as John, my sweet but always tactful husband, puts it — "discuss anything and everything."

Women also have the need to interact without the judgment and petty competition inherent in some women's groups. At FAC I can show up on a bad-hair day with chipped nail polish and unshaven legs and know I won't be the talk of the PTA. And, even though I'm known by fans of my column as a cross between the industrious "Fly Lady" and the unsinkable "Martha," my FAC friends promise to carry the secret of my peeling wallpaper and disorganized drawers to their graves.

Secret keeping aside, investing in friend-

21

ship with a supportive group of women has produced returns I never could have imagined. As our kids grew up, so did FAC. Now, in the midst of jokes about Botox and drooping derrieres, we stretch and encourage one another. We've also discovered an important truth. It's much easier to wade through difficult times locking arms with those who love you even without lipstick or a great cheesecake recipe.

So, when I picked up the message that FAC was at Jessie's house this afternoon, I knew I'd be there — early. The leash on my hag had begun to unravel even before I'd stepped out of bed that morning . . .

I woke up to the hot, moist breath of the family dog on my cheek. Over the past five years, Daisy has learned that panting in my face is an extremely effective way to get me out of bed. If I don't move quickly, she starts to lick my ear. Just the thought of that scavenging dog's tongue lapping at my ear makes me cringe. Who knows what she's been licking five minutes earlier? Ugh! I still don't understand why Daisy adopted me as her morning pal. I never wanted a dog in the first place. It was John who felt the responsibility of caring for a pet would be good for the kids. I suggested a goldfish. He suggested a hamster. That did it. The threat of a rodent moving into our home made me agree to a dog. I could just imagine the unpleasant dreams that would haunt me with a rodent spinning a wheel in the next room. After all, I had seen the movie *Willard.*

Today I knew there was trouble, because I smelled cinnamon. Not the good kind of cinnamon from baking bread or rolls but a cloyingly sweet smell, like those little red-hot candies. Daisy's breath may smell like many things — most of which are too disgusting even to mention — but cinnamon has not yet popped up on the list. I opened my eyes to discover that the source of the smell was not only emanating from her mouth but from red goo smeared in various places throughout her white fur. In my post-dreamlike state, she resembled some fantasy creature from *The Wizard of Oz.*

I emerged from under my comforter (now spotted with the mystery substance), gingerly picked up the slimy dog, and followed the path of pink paw prints to the hall bathroom. There I found red toothpaste smeared all over the floor and spied the chewed-up plastic tube behind the toilet.

"Katie! Josh! Hannah!" I shouted. "Upstairs! Now!"

I was definitely using what we refer to in our home as an "outdoor voice." I learned this term as a naive, young mother by listening to Katie's preschool teacher reprimand a student for shouting in class. The scene is somehow set permanently in my memory . . .

"Billy, is that your 'indoor' voice?" Mrs. Stevens asked sweetly that day.

"I don't know," he responded, clearly only interested in continuing his raucous romp through the cardboard bricks of the Building My World discovery center.

"Remember our rules," she persisted. "We save loud voices for outdoors and use quiet voices indoors. You don't want me to write your name in *The Book* for breaking the rules, do you?"

Just the mention of *The Book* stopped this wild child in his tracks. "No, Mrs. Stevens," he replied in an apparently repentant fashion.

Wow! I recall the ear-shattering level of noise in my own home. *Why have I never heard about this indoor-outdoor voice rule? Maybe getting my own copy of* The Book *will lower the decibels.*

Ever hopeful, I stopped at the stationery store on the way home.

■ ■ ■ ■

Unfortunately, *The Book* worked much more effectively in Mrs. Stevens's classroom. The first time I threatened *The Book,* Katie eyed me quizzically and my husband started laughing. It wasn't long before we began to use *The Book* as a notepad for phone messages.

Consequently, as I waited in the hall, holding a slippery dog, it dawned on me that I would probably hear about this breach of self-control from my children the next time I brought up the indoor-voice subject. But at that point, with cinnamon toothpaste smeared on the front of my nightgown, I didn't care. I suspected that even the serene, pearl-wearing June Cleaver would employ her outdoor voice in this situation.

Katie was the first to poke her head out of the bedroom in response to my call. "What's the problem, Mom? I'm already late."

I was not surprised. Katie, a typical seventeen-year-old girl, was always running late for school. After all, it takes time to choose and discard a minimum of four complete outfits before finding that "perfect" T-shirt and pair of sweatpants in which to roam the halls of her high school. And

25

this doesn't include the lengthy process of straightening her already sleek blond tresses with a flatiron to erase even the slightest hint of a "lump." Every time I got irritated with her habits, I tried to remind myself that, yes, I, too, was once a teenage girl. But was I really that annoying, that self-focused? Or had the years simply wiped away my memory, along with my high-school figure?

Taking a deep cleansing breath to compose myself, I held up our gooey, red-spotted pet. "Explain this, please."

"What?" asked my oldest child as she emerged from her room to cautiously examine the dog. "Oh, that. Josh stepped on the toothpaste last night and — of course — didn't clean it up. Daisy must have gotten into it."

"Don't *even* try to blame this on me!" hollered my fifteen-year-old son from the staircase.

At six-foot-one and still growing, Josh is like a puppy who hasn't grown into his paws yet. Big and unwieldy, he tumbles headfirst into a situation.

"I only stepped on the toothpaste because *she* knocked it on the floor with the cord to the blow-dryer," Josh countered, shaking his red head vehemently. "You gotta talk to her, Mom. Her stuff is all over the bathroom and —"

"It is not! And I didn't even know it fell off the counter, bratface!"

"All right, stop with the name-calling," I interjected. "Josh, let me get this straight. You saw the toothpaste on the floor without a cap and decided to just leave it there?"

"No, I already told you. I told Katie to pick it up."

Katie's cobalt eyes narrowed to slits. "Not before I told *you* to *clean* it up after you stomped on the tube with your big feet and squirted toothpaste all over!"

"Back off, Barbie doll! There wouldn't have been anything to clean up if you hadn't —"

A horn blared from outside the house.

"Gotta go, Mom! There's my ride!" Josh bounded down the stairs and out the door before I could utter a sound.

"Mommy, the tile was all pink and sticky when I went to bed," said our younger daughter, appearing magically from around the corner. Confident she wasn't in trouble, she added sweetly, "That's why I used your bathroom."

At ten years old, Hannah has mastered the fine art of sucking up. With her deep blue eyes, pudgy cheeks, and cap of strawberry blond curls, she looks like a cherub.

Hovering on the sidelines, she listens for an opportune time to jump in with a helpful suggestion or juicy piece of information gathered through surreptitious surveillance of her older siblings. Unfortunately, in this instance, she had misinterpreted the situation.

I took another cleansing breath. "Hannah, why didn't you tell me last night that toothpaste was all over the bathroom floor?"

The startled look on her face showed that she quickly realized her miscalculation. "I don't know," she said and disappeared behind her swiftly closing bedroom door.

I sighed. "OK, Kate." I swiveled to face my older daughter again and held the dog out to her. "I need you to clean up the bathroom floor and give the dog a bath. I'll follow the paw prints and assess the rest of the damage."

"Now? You're asking me to do this *now? * Right *now? * This *morning? * Before *school? * Without giving me any *warning? * Mom, you *know* that's not fair!" she wailed, backing away from me and a squirming Daisy. "This was *not* my fault, and you *know* it! Besides, I'm already dressed! I won't have time to change before the first bell!"

"Then you'll be late," I responded, proud of my indoor voice.

"Mom! I *can't* be late! We have a *math* test first hour," she continued to wail.

"You'll have to make it up."

"Ms. Murray gives us a *zero* unless we have a valid excuse."

"I'll write you a note."

"Yeah, like cleaning the bathroom is a 'valid' excuse."

I paused. A chink in my armor.

It must have showed.

"You'd have to say I was sick or something," Katie continued. "Do you really feel it's right to *lie* to my teacher, Mom?"

"Fine. Just go to school." I sighed again, accepting my defeat — and headed to the shower with the dog under my arm.

Let's just say that a bath of any kind is *never* in Daisy's plans . . . much less a shower.

And all this was at 7:30 a.m. Before things *really* started to go downhill.

By ten o'clock I had discovered a mistake in the checkbook register. Our account was in overdraft mode, making it likely that our tithe to the church would bounce. I tried unsuccessfully for ninety minutes to make an online transfer from our savings account to cover the discrepancy. No matter what I did, a warning code popped up on the screen to inform me that I had "entered an unauthorized access number. Please try again."

"You're wrong!" I shouted at the computer monitor. "This is the right access code, you useless box of megabytes! Who else would know the combination of my current dress size and the size I'm planning to be by summer vacation?"

I despise computers when they won't do what I want. I also despise admitting that I can't get the blasted machines to do what I want. But what I truly despise the most is letting my husband know that I can't get the computer to do what I want. I suspect this could be traced to some unresolved "I am woman! Hear me roar!" female consciousness raising course from my college days.

Thus it took several more minutes of yelling at the computer and pounding on the table before I swallowed my pride and called my husband at his office.

"Oh, by the way, John," I casually mentioned after a few minutes of trumped-up small talk to hide my real reason for the call. "I was trying to make a transfer online, and the bank won't accept our access code."

"What are you trying to do?"

"I told you. I'm trying to make a transfer."

There was a pause on the other end of the phone line, then the puzzled question, "Why do you need to make a transfer?"

"Sweetheart, we don't have time to get into all this now," I said, trying desperately to keep the word *overdraft* out of our conversation. "Did you change the access code recently?"

"Umm . . . I don't think so. But, Liz, why do you need —"

"Wait! I might be getting another call," I chirped before he had a chance to realize I was trying to avoid his question. "Better go — it could be the kids. Don't worry, honey. I'll figure it out. See you at dinner!"

Once again, saved by the specter of call waiting. Meanwhile our account was still in overdraft and the hag was pulling at her leash.

I wasted another precious thirty minutes attempting to navigate our bank's "timesaving" voice-mail system in an effort to explain my problem to a real person. I finally gave up and drove to the bank to make the deposit. Because it was ten minutes after noon, the cheery teller behind the bulletproof glass in the drive-through reminded me that the transfer would not be credited to our account until the next business day. Monday.

"But what if a check goes through today or on Saturday?" I asked.

"No problem," she reassured me. "You have overdraft protection."

"Wonderful." Relieved, I extracted the deposit receipt from the mechanical tray.

But then the teller continued, "The overdraft fee of thirty-five dollars per check will be automatically charged to your account. Is there anything else I can help you with?"

Before the hag could crane her wrinkled neck out the window and inform the teller (in an outdoor voice) how she felt about the bank's overdraft-protection plan, I stepped on the gas.

It was now 12:30, and any resolve to stay on my low-carb diet was running dangerously low. By 1:15, I'd pulled out of Krispy Kreme, brushing the glistening remains of two glazed "hot and ready" donuts from my sweater.

"Oh no! Today is Hannah's parent lunch!" I exclaim, slapping my forehead and causing the driver in the next car to roll up his window. I'm now convinced my daughter will someday reveal this — and other lapses of maternal care — on national television before a gray-haired Oprah.

Little did I know that Oprah was the least of my worries.

Armed with a double mocha frappuccino, I arrived to pick up Hannah from school promptly at 2:15.

"Hi, sweetheart! How was your day?" I said in that high, overly cheerful voice used by guilt-ridden mothers.

Stony silence.

Undaunted, I pushed on. "I picked this up for you," I continued to chirp, handing her the whipped-cream-topped bribe. "It's a double mocha — and I even had them put chocolate shavings on top for you."

"Katie says chocolate will give me zits," she fired back.

"Hannah, sweetheart, you have gorgeous skin!" I gushed. "You don't have to worry about blemishes. Besides, my dermatologist told me that whole chocolate thing is just a myth."

"Maybe for OLD skin," she said with a pointed look as she climbed into the backseat of the van and put on her headphones — a definite signal that a double mocha frappuccino was not even close to the penance she was planning for me. I'd probably end up making her a whole batch of her favorite cookies, which I have come to call

I'm-So-Sorry Snickerdoodles.

After dropping a ticked-off Hannah at dance lessons, I returned home to find that cinnamon toothpaste does not agree with Daisy. I spent the next thirty minutes and half a tub of OxyBooster trying to remove pink vomit from our beige carpeting. The attempt was unsuccessful, so I gave up and covered the spot with a rug. I cringe just thinking about what fans of my column would think if they could see their domestic diva now.

By the time I had put away my cleaning supplies, the hag was seething and more than ready to pounce on the first person through the door. I picked up Jessie's voice mail inviting me to Friday Afternoon Club just in time.

■ ■ ■ ■

CHAPTER TWO

■ ■ ■ ■

Jessie's Raspberry Tea

1 quart strong brewed tea
1 (10 oz.) package frozen raspberries
1 (12 oz.) can frozen lemonade

Instructions

1. Stir frozen raspberries and lemonade into warm tea until thawed.
2. Fill a two-quart pitcher with ice. Strain mixture over ice and add water to fill pitcher.
3. Enjoy in tall glasses, garnished with a sprig of mint.

Marina's Tabbouleh

1/2 cup bulgur (also known as cracked wheat)
1 bunch of fresh mint, chopped
2 bunches of flat-leafed parsley, chopped
1 small onion, finely chopped

2 medium Roma tomatoes, diced
Juice of one lemon
3 tablespoons olive oil
Salt and pepper to taste
Optional: Seven Spices seasoning
  (sometimes called Syrian Spices)

Instructions

1. Soak bulgur in warm water for 30 minutes. Drain.
2. Add all ingredients together. Season to taste.

I walk into Jessie's chaotic kitchen about 3:30. Jess homeschools her four kids, so there is always some project drying, growing, or festering on her counters. She's one of the few women who has a valid excuse for "science projects" in her refrigerator.

We can't help but tease Jessie about being born in the wrong generation. She's the quintessential '70s earth mother — complete with waist-length hair, huge organic garden, golden retriever, and clogs. She may be a misplaced flower child, but when it comes to needing an anchor in the midst of a storm, we all flock to Jessie.

One look at my face and Jess says, "Tell me."

She sets two glasses of raspberry tea on her long, oak kitchen table and slides into the chair next to me.

"Really, it's nothing. Just a rotten day. It sounds silly now."

"Tell me."

"All right, I'll give you the short version. Red goo. Sticky dog. Uncooperative kids. Bank overdrafts. Computer problems. All shaken up with maternal guilt, chocolate, zits, and pink vomit."

Jess smiles. "Sounds like the perfect day."

"I just needed a break. I'm so glad you called."

"Me too. Cheers!"

We clink glasses. I'm feeling better already.

"Hey! Don't you two dare start without me!" roars Marina, bursting through the back door. She's still in uniform and clutching what looks like a bouquet of weeds.

Marina is a single mom who works the day shift as a cop for the Omaha Police Department. With her wild black hair and fiery red acrylic fingernails, she definitely breaks the "Joe Friday" mold.

I once asked if she thought her flamboyant image might affect her credibility on the job.

"Of course it does," she had replied. "Most men don't take me seriously. It's my advantage." That's Marina.

"What'd you do, Rina? Hop the fence?" asks Jess.

As a lieutenant on the force, Marina spends less time on the street and more time, as she says, "pushing paper and listening to whiny cops." But with her wiry, athletic body, I have little doubt she could easily sail over the picket fence between her and Jess's yards.

"Are you kidding?" She laughs. "Those days are over, girlfriend. By the way, I hope it was OK to steal some of the mint from your backyard, Jess."

"Please, pick all you want. It's taking over the garden," laments Jessie.

"What are you going to do with all that mint?" I ask, as Marina tosses the spray of greenery on the already-cluttered counter.

"I thought I'd mix up some tabbouleh for the OPD spring picnic this weekend. Those cops need to expand their palates beyond burgers and macaroni salad."

Jess's golden retriever, Max, jumps at the sound of the bell. Before she can grab his collar, he bounds toward the front door.

"That must be Mary Alice." Jess rises from her chair. "I've told her for years to just come on in, but she's too polite."

"Not when she's with me! I'll wrench her out of that comfort zone yet," says Kelly, the youngest member of our group, as she strides into the kitchen. She plops a platter loaded with cheese cubes and fresh vegetables in the center of the table. "I come bearing treats, ladies."

At five-foot-two, Kelly may be tiny, but her presence fills a room as soon as she walks through the door. Her quick smile, deep auburn hair, and smattering of freckles belie a will of iron.

As Kelly removes the plastic wrap from the tray, Mary Alice walks into the room. "Good boy, Max." She rubs the old dog's

41

neck. "Is Kelly taking credit for my cooking again?"

"What cooking?" Kelly insists. "It's veggies and cheese. Since when does filling up a platter with store-bought crudités constitute cooking?"

"It's all in the presentation, you peasant!" Jess laughs, throwing her arm around Mary Alice's shoulder and giving her a reassuring hug.

"Thank you, Jess," says Mary Alice. "And for your information, Kel, I made the dip."

This fact does not surprise me at all. Mary Alice most likely inspired the phrase "busy hands — peaceful heart." I marvel at how, with three active kids, she has time to do it all — cook, keep a spotless house, and always look "put together." She wouldn't think about leaving the house without applying her characteristic rose-colored lipstick and making sure her sleek brown hair is in place. Much like the TV commercial, when something "absolutely, positively" needs to get done, call Mary Alice. She is an organizational wizard without a procrastinating bone in her body. Naturally, we all hate her.

"This green stuff is supposed to be a dip?" Kelly jokes. "Seriously, this looks great, M.A., and it's low carb."

Marina wrinkles her nose. "Yada, yada, yada . . . I am sick to death of hearing the carbohydrate count of every food worth eating. In my opinion, life without pasta is just not worth living."

After a few minutes of debate about the pros and cons of various popular diets, I decide to change the subject before my trip to Krispy Kreme comes up. I ask about the sixth member of our little group. "Jess, is Lucy coming? I was really hoping she'd be here. I haven't seen her for weeks."

"I don't know. I called and left a message. I even sent her an e-mail. It's not like Lucy not to respond."

"She's been keeping to herself since her mom died last spring," says Mary Alice. "I'm starting to worry about her."

Kelly frowns. "That's been six months. She needs to get out — be around people."

"Then let's go get her," says Marina. "She can't stand us up three weeks in a row. Don't we have something against that in our bylaws?"

"FAC doesn't have bylaws, Marina," Kelly reminds her.

"Then I guess we'll have to do an unofficial FAC intervention."

"What's an 'intervention'?" asks Mary Alice.

"I don't know yet. We'll figure it out on the way. In the car, ladies . . . I'm driving." Clearly a woman used to giving orders.

"Are you sure, Rina? Maybe she still wants some time alone," persists Mary Alice.

"That's the point. She doesn't need time alone — she needs FAC. Let's go!"

"I agree. Grab the food." Kelly heads for the door.

"I've got the tea." I suspect we'll need all the carbs we can get in the next couple of hours.

■ ■ ■ ■

CHAPTER THREE

■ ■ ■ ■

AUNT BETTE'S CREAM BISCUITS

2 cups all-purpose flour
1 tablespoon baking powder
3 tablespoons sugar
1/2 teaspoon salt
1 1/4 cups heavy cream

Instructions

1. Sift flour, baking powder, sugar, and salt together in a bowl.
2. Add cream and stir gently just until a dough forms.
3. Gather dough into a ball and knead gently a few times on a lightly floured surface. Gently roll out 1/2 inch thick.
4. Cut dough with biscuit cutter or into squares. Brush tops with cream.
5. Bake on an ungreased baking sheet

at 425 degrees for 15 minutes, or until light golden brown.

6. Cool on a rack for about 5 minutes.

Cherry Preserves

2 lbs. sour cherries (weight after pits removed)
1 1/2 lbs. sugar

Instructions

1. Add sugar to pitted cherries.
2. Bring mixture to a rolling boil over medium-high heat.
3. Cook until fruit mixture is clear, skimming, if necessary.
4. Pour immediately into clean hot jars and seal according to manufacturer's instructions.

When we arrive at Lucy's, I'm the first one out of the car. As I climb the porch steps and peer into her large front-room window, I'm appalled at what I see.

Lucy is curled under a blanket on the sofa, flipping through the TV channels. A small platoon of dirty glasses sits in formation on the table behind her. Paper plates, tissues, and newspapers litter the coffee table in front.

Lucy's normally pale skin appears almost translucent — a stark contrast to the dark under-eye circles. Although it's 4:00 in the afternoon, she is wearing a loose flannel nightgown and mismatched socks. I am more than a little shocked to see her normally tidy, blond pageboy pulled back with what looks like an uncoated red rubber band that bears a strong resemblance to the type my son Josh uses to bundle the newspapers before his route.

When I ring the doorbell, Lucy turns away. Apparently she intends to ignore the noise — that is, until she hears Marina's unmistakable voice.

"Police! Open up! We know you're in there, Lucy!"

I silently pray that Lucy answers the door before the neighbors emerge from their homes to see what's going on. I breathe a sigh of relief as I notice a small smile tease at the corner of her mouth. She pulls herself off the sofa, wrapping the blanket around her thin body, and opens the door.

"Thank you very much, Marina," says Lucy with what I hope is mock irritation. "You've given the busybodies on the block something to talk about for the next few months."

"No problem. This neighborhood needs a little excitement," Marina retorts. She pushes the door open wider and bulldozes her way into the house.

An apologetic-looking Mary Alice, carrying her tray of appetizers, follows Marina. "It was her idea," she whispers to Lucy, then scurries after our brazen friend.

Kelly steps through the door into the foyer. "Lucy, we thought it was time for an intervention."

"And we miss you," adds Jess, gathering Lucy close in a hug.

"Ladies, I hate to interrupt this love fest, but this pitcher of tea is sweating all over my new shoes," I complain, scooting past the group to the kitchen.

As I look around, I see that Lucy's normally well-kept home has the dusty film of neglect. Mail is stacked in several piles that are toppling over on the kitchen counter.

Car keys lie on the floor of the adjoining mud room next to a jacket and a pair of shoes. The sliding trash bin under the sink is partly open, and it's overflowing with empty yogurt cartons and soup cans.

Good thing she doesn't have a dog.

Mary Alice carries an armload of paper plates and assorted trash from the family room into the kitchen.

"There's no room." I point to the trash. "I'll take it to the garage."

"No, I'll do it." Stepping closer, she whispers, "Liz, I can't believe this place. Now I'm really worried. This isn't Lucy. I feel terrible about not checking on her sooner."

"The last thing Lucy needs is you overflowing with guilt," Kelly warns, joining us in the kitchen. "That'll make her feel worse. We're here now, and this time we're not leaving until she changes out of that ratty nightgown and turns off the television."

I wipe the pitcher of tea with a dishtowel and carry it and a stack of paper cups to the den. Apparently too edgy to sit down, Mary Alice begins to fold blankets and plump cushions. Out of the corner of my eye, I see Kelly raise her eyebrows in a "Stop it!" look directed at Mary Alice.

"I hope it's OK to use these," I say, hold-

51

ing up the cups. "I couldn't find any glasses in the cupboard."

"Oh, I know the place is a mess." Lucy is once again huddled under a blanket on the sofa. With her long legs folded to her chest, she looks like a shrunken version of her former self.

At five-foot-nine, Lucy is one of those girls you pitied in seventh grade because she was taller than most of the boys. Then, in high school, your pity turned to envy when the captain of the basketball team asked her to the prom.

A picture of a gray-templed Judd, her basketball-star husband, sits on the bookshelf among several framed photographs chronicling their life together. Judd, the senior vice president of a large communications firm, had died just over a year and a half ago in the fiery crash of the small charter plane he was piloting.

After the plane crash, Lucy had been a pillar of grace and strength. She had guided their only child, Allison, through the last few months of her senior year in high school, convincing her that her daddy would have wanted her to enjoy this special time of her life.

When Alli had left for college, Lucy had assumed around-the-clock care for her mother, whose cancer had spread to the brain. Again Lucy's strength seemed to flow from what appeared to be a never-ending fount.

Her church group had seemed to understand when she quit the weekly Bible study she had attended for several years. "After all, she has so much on her plate," one of the members told me when we ran into each other at the grocery store. She'd added that Lucy's strength was a powerful testimony to the others in the group.

But when Lucy had buried her mother last spring, she told us she felt like a light inside her had been extinguished. She had no desire to get out of bed in the morning, much less venture out the door. We reminded her that she'd been through an enormous amount of trauma. It would take time to grieve — and even longer to heal. As a licensed family therapist, Kelly had explained the grief process, assured Lucy that her feelings were normal, and encouraged her to resume a normal schedule as soon as possible.

Instead, without telling anyone, Lucy had decided to turn her leave of absence from volunteer work with at-risk teens at the Hope Center into a resignation. Through mutual friends, we found out that she seldom accepted invitations to lunch or other events. She had quit answering e-mail and apparently was screening her phone calls. I also heard that Lucy still hadn't returned to her Bible study group.

I suspected that most of the people in Lucy's circle were afraid to approach her, especially regarding her apparently self-imposed seclusion. With so much tragedy, it's difficult to know what to say. Often friends find it easier to accept unanswered messages as a signal that a person needs time alone.

This wasn't the case with FAC. We knew Lucy. And the woman huddled on the sofa needed a loving — but serious — shove.

"All right, ladies, let's quit dancing around the issue," begins Marina, turning to face Lucy on the sofa. "Luce, you look terrible. This place is a mess. And I'm ready to start flaming you if I don't get a response to my e-mail. If you think we are gonna let you sit here the rest of your life watching the Lifetime channel, you've got another think coming."

"Besides, Lucy, we miss you," says Mary Alice. "I know *I* do."

"A lot of people miss you," adds Kelly. "The girls at the Hope Center ask me all the time when that tall, skinny lady who coached their volleyball team is coming back. And, to be honest, it's beginning to grate on me. I may be short, but I have a killer serve."

Lucy rubs her temples. "I'm sorry, Kelly. I miss the girls at the Hope Center too."

"Then what are you doing here in your jammies clutching the remote?" Marina asks.

A flash of anger lights up Lucy's cool, blue eyes. "I want you to know — all of you — that I haven't been just sitting here watching television. I've been very busy. Have any of you ever closed an estate?"

"No, but —," Kelly begins.

Lucy interrupts. "Remember, I'm an only child, so everything's left to me. There are a lot of decisions to make . . . a lot of loose ends . . ." Tears begin to slip down her cheeks.

That did it. The five of us rush over, pulling her into a group hug and scattering Mary Alice's appetizer tray all over the antique oriental carpet that covers Lucy's polished wood floors.

"Oh!" we cry in unison, jumping back to avoid the mess.

"Lucy, I'm so sorry. Look at your carpet." Mary Alice tries to trap a cherry tomato with her toe before it rolls under the sofa.

"Forget about it," says Lucy. "I need a hug much more than a clean carpet."

Trying not to squash the cheese cubes into the rug, we tumble into a group embrace, grateful we are at Lucy's house, where no family members are present to witness our emotional display.

I've seen this kind of female "pack" behavior actually cause my husband to break out in a cold sweat. He shifts from foot to foot, rubbing his hands on the front of his jeans, not sure whether to intervene or sneak out the back door. The kids react differently — crowding together in a little gaggle. They roll their eyes but secretly file the information away to bring up at an opportune time.

After making our way through a box of tissues and sweeping up the remains of the doomed appetizer tray, we settle in Lucy's comfortable family room with a glass of raspberry tea, courtesy of the ever-vigilant Mary Alice. Jess sits on the sofa near Lucy, resting an arm protectively around her shoulders. Kelly and Marina position themselves in chairs on either side, like eager *Jeopardy* contestants poised for the next question.

I'm grateful that, for once, Mary Alice seems content to sit relatively still on the edge of the hearth instead of darting around the room picking up dishes or looking for something to fluff. I sink back into the soft leather of what Lucy still refers to as "Judd's chair," feeling overwhelmed by the enormity of her situation and without a clue of what to say or do to help. I needn't have worried.

Kelly takes charge. "Let's start by making a list of all the decisions you have to make. The process is less overwhelming when you put it on paper."

"I love lists!" Mary Alice fishes out the pen and notebook she keeps in her purse.

Marina rolls her eyes my way with a look that clearly communicates, *You'd better control her, or I'm gonna pull out my handcuffs.*

"I really don't feel like going into it right now," protests Lucy. "I'm so tired today. Maybe after the weekend."

"Low energy," says Marina. "A definite sign of carbohydrate deficiency. I always keep a few candy bars in the glove compartment for emergencies. I'll run out and grab a few."

"No, please don't bother, Marina," Lucy begins. "I'm really not hungry, and my stomach has been bothering me."

"This has nothing to do with hunger," counters Marina. "Chocolate is medicinal — almost a miracle food. Haven't you heard the reports about all the nutrients in the cocoa bean? Chocolate's good for every-thing from mood swings to heart disease."

"Is that true, Jess?" It's clear Mary Alice doubts the veracity of Marina's research on the subject.

"I did read something on the Web about the benefits of dark chocolate," replies Jess. "I just can't remember the details."

"How come I haven't heard about this?" I pipe up, secretly wondering if my children purposely hid this information from me so they could keep all the holiday candy to themselves.

"Let's stick to the subject, shall we, ladies?" Kelly holds up her hands in an ap-parent effort to head off what could likely turn into a spirited discussion on the anti-oxidant properties of the cocoa bean. "I promise we can break out the chocolate later."

"I've heard that before," I mutter under my breath.

"Focus, ladies," scolds Kelly. "Now, Lucy, what are the most pressing decisions you have to make?"

"Where do you want me to start? Real estate? Investments? Retirement? Insurance? I can go on and on. That's the problem . . . there's just so much. And there's only me. I don't know anything about these areas. Judd used to . . . What if I make a mistake?"

Jess sighs. "Oh, Lucy. It breaks my heart that you have to go through this . . . but that's the reality of the situation."

"She's right, Luce," says Marina. "You can't just shut out the world. You have to take charge."

"But I don't even know where to begin."

"Since you mentioned it first, let's start with real estate." Kelly makes a note on the pad Mary Alice had set neatly in front of her. "What do you own?"

"Well, of course, this house. Then there's Mother's home, Dad's old fishing cabin. And to complicate things further, a letter arrived the other day from my mother's aunt, telling me she's decided to move into a retirement community."

"What does that have to do with you?" asks Marina. "Do you need to help her move? If so, I can round up some guys from the station."

"Oh, Rina, I hadn't even thought about that! I suppose she will need some help. Aunt Bette must be over ninety years old by now — but you'd never guess it. She has always been so independent."

"My grandmother was the same way." Jess laughs. "The only way we could convince her to give up the car keys was by promising to buy her a golf cart. She zips all over town with that thing . . . and it drives my mom crazy."

"You're kidding!" I say. "She drives a golf cart?"

"That's right. I've told Mom to quit worrying about her, Gram can't do too much damage when the golf cart won't top 20 mph."

"My grandmother never learned to drive," Mary Alice adds, "and neither did my mom. She seemed content letting Daddy take her where she needed to go."

"The good old days . . . before the curse of carpool and soccer practice," I muse.

"Once again, ladies, we're getting off the topic," Kelly reminds us. "So, Lucy, what does your aunt's moving into a retirement home have to do with settling your mom's estate?"

"In her letter, Aunt Bette told me that the house she lived in all these years actually belonged to Mother. So now that Mother's gone, it has passed to me. All this time I had no idea she owned the house."

"She never brought it up?" I ask.

"Not that I recall. Mother rarely spoke about her side of the family. I do remember visiting Aunt Bette's house as a child. She would set a beautiful table with a steaming pot of tea, fresh cream biscuits, and home-made cherry preserves from her tree in the backyard. It was a real tea party."

"That's so sweet," says Jess.

"This talk about biscuits is making me hungry." Marina rubs her stomach. "What's the difference between cream biscuits and the kind in the can?"

"Don't worry about it." I elbow Marina playfully. "You'll never try the recipe. You'd have to buy a rolling pin."

"Hey, 'Martha,' I can always use my night-stick."

"Shh!" admonishes Kelly, in another attempt to get us back on track. "Is the house here in Omaha, Lucy?"

"No, it's just outside some little town in southeast Nebraska. Tredway, I think it's called."

Kelly raises an eyebrow. "I've never heard of it."

"Me neither," says Marina. "Are you sure that's the name? I used to patrol Hall County when I was a state trooper. I don't remember a Tredway."

"It's about sixty miles south of here. Near the Missouri border in Cramer County."

"Oh, that Tredway!" Memories of my college days as a cub reporter flood back. "I did an internship at the newspaper in Orrick, just west of the town on Highway 9. Tredway is the county seat, isn't it?"

"I'm sorry, Liz. I haven't the slightest idea. As I said, I only visited a few times as a child."

"From what I remember, there are some neat old houses in the area."

"I'm sure we're talking about the same place. I remember Aunt Bette saying she and my grandfather were born in the house. That means it has to be at least a hundred years old."

"I wouldn't be surprised if it's a lot older. Much of the area was settled before the Civil War."

"I didn't know you were such a history buff, Liz," says Jess.

"The more accurate term would be *gofer.* I spent most of my internship at the library doing research for the 'real' reporters — all three of them. Cramer County was celebrating its 125th birthday at the time, and the paper did a series of stories to commemorate."

"I love small towns," comments Mary Alice. "Especially the ones that still have those neat town squares with a café and little shops. I think I could retire in a small town."

"Not me. I'm a city girl," says Marina. "I'd be lost without the mall and a ready source of lattes."

"Shallow!" I tease.

Kelly clears her throat. "So, Lucy, would you like to keep this property or sell it?"

"Truthfully, Kelly, I'd like it to just disappear. I don't have the energy to deal with it."

"You know that's not an option, Lucy. But you can hire a real-estate broker to get it ready for market and handle the sale."

Lucy's brow wrinkles in thought. "On the other hand, I'd hate to see the property be sold to some stranger. There's a lot of family history there."

"What about other family members?" asks Jess. "Would any of them be interested in buying it?"

"Mother had one brother, but he was killed in the Korean War . . . and Aunt Bette never married."

Mary Alice leans forward. "What does Alli think, Lucy?"

"The letter just came last week. I haven't even brought it up to her. She has enough on her plate at school."

"Lucy, whether Alli realizes it or not, the house is part of her history," says Jess. "Don't you think she should at least have a say in what you do?"

"You're probably right, but I have no idea

what shape the property is in. I'm sure Mother visited Aunt Bette, but I haven't been there in years."

"That settles it then," Marina states, as if the decision is a done deal. "The only way to find out what kind of shape the house is in is to take a look at it. I say we have FAC in Tredway next week."

"From what I remember about Aunt Bette, I'm sure she'd love to have us," says Lucy. "But, honestly, I don't think I'm ready."

Kelly squeezes Lucy's hand. "No one ever feels ready to deal with painful memories. But you're going to have to face them eventually."

"Remember," adds Jess, "we'll be right there, praying you through it."

Tears began to slip down Lucy's cheeks again. "All right, we'll go to Tredway — soon. But I have one condition. Marina has to drive. I think I'm going to need those candy bars in the glove compartment."

CHAPTER FOUR

Clarenzo's Brasciole

1 (2–2 1/2 lbs.) round steak (ask butcher to butterfly the meat)
Rind of one lemon, grated
Salt and pepper to taste
2 1/2 teaspoons oregano
1/4 lb. prosciutto, thinly sliced
4 eggs, hardboiled, peeled and chopped
2 cups bread crumbs
1/2 cup Parmesan cheese, grated
1/2 cup chopped parsley
1/2 teaspoon dried rosemary (crumbled between fingers)
1/2 cup flour
1/4 cup olive oil
4 cloves of garlic, minced
1 small onion, chopped
1/2 cup dry red wine
2 cups chopped, canned pear tomatoes, undrained

Instructions

1. Open butterflied steak and pound between plastic with a meat mallet until 1/4 inch thick.
2. Rub meat with lemon rind, salt, pepper, and 1 1/2 teaspoons oregano.
3. Lay prosciutto slices evenly on steak. Sprinkle evenly with chopped egg, bread crumbs, grated Parmesan, and parsley.
4. Roll up meat tightly, taking care to tuck in both ends to hold in filling while cooking. Tie roll with string at 2-inch intervals.
5. Season flour with rosemary, remaining oregano, salt and pepper. Rub this mixture onto surface of beef roll.
6. Brown meat roll in olive oil in a large pan over medium-high heat.
7. Add garlic and onion to the pan and sauté until it begins to brown.
8. Add wine, and cook for one minute.
9. Add tomatoes with their juice. Cover pan and simmer over low heat for 1 1/2 hours, or until meat is very tender. Add wine as needed to keep liquid in pan.

10. Remove meat from pan, remove strings and cut into 1-inch-thick slices. Pour tomato mixture over the slices. Serves 4–6.

Drucillina's Death By Chocolate

8 oz. dark semisweet chocolate
2/3 cup butter
1 cup sugar
4 large eggs
1/2 cup flour
4 tablespoons unsweetened cocoa powder
2 teaspoons baking powder
1 teaspoon vanilla extract
1/4 cup sour cream

Instructions

1. Preheat oven to 350 degrees.
2. Line bottom of a 9-inch round cake pan with a circle of parchment paper. Grease sides of pan.
3. Break chocolate into small pieces. Gently melt it with butter in a pan over hot water or in the microwave.
4. Beat eggs with sugar until well combined and slightly thickened. Mix in flour, cocoa powder, baking powder, and vanilla extract.
5. Slowly fold in sour cream and

melted chocolate mixture.

6. Bake at 350 degrees for 50 minutes, or until a wooden pick inserted in center comes out clean.
7. Cool cake. Remove from pan and peel off parchment paper. Frost with chocolate ganache.

Chocolate Ganache Frosting

1. Gently heat 2/3 cup heavy cream in a saucepan, or microwave.
2. Add 9 oz. chopped dark semisweet chocolate. Stir until smooth. Pour over cake.

It always amazes me how time flies during FAC! Now that our little "intervention" with Lucy was over, we spent the last hour in typical female fashion — talking about nothing. That's what is so great about getting together with girlfriends. You don't need the distraction of a "topic" for conversation to flow. In fact, most of the time, we all talk at once — switching conversations like corn popping in a kettle. While such interactions are second nature to most women, this drives men crazy.

My dear husband once commented after coming home from work early and witnessing the tail end of a particularly lively FAC at our house that he couldn't understand how women seem to enjoy "talking everything to death." I responded by pointing out he should consider FAC a blessing for providing an alternative audience. That raised a male eyebrow. And then I went as far as suggesting he look at FAC not as just a female diversion, but as the true marriage-building activity it is. By this comment I was starting to get around to the fact that it may be a wee bit taxing for the average man to have to absorb *all* of a woman's words.

I once read an article about "a woman's word count" and "a man's word count," which explained just how many words each gender requires during an average day. The author of the article (a man!) said that most men complete their required word count during the "normal workday" — even before they get home to their families. It seems they are talked out before they walk through the door. And this is the time when most women are chomping at the bit for meaningful communication — or just plain chatter.

Until I read this article, I was sure John's "hmms" and grunts, which he refers to as "filtering," was an indication he needed more practice in the art of communication. My response was to try to draw him out — by talking more. And more. After I came across that article, I understood why John failed to get "better" at the art of conversation when he was getting so much practice. I couldn't wait to tell him about my discovery when he got home, but all he said was "hmm."

John was true to form in this instance. Apparently sensing that this subject was on the verge of being talked to death, he suddenly remembered something he had to attend to in the garage. I've never seen a faster exit . . .

"I hate to break things up, ladies," says Jess, pulling my mind back to the present, "but I need to get home. Michael and I have a date night."

"Oooohhhh," we tease.

"I expect it to be quite the evening. Look, I even painted my toenails." Jess stretches out a manicured foot for inspection.

"I have plans, too, but my evening won't be quite so exciting," Kelly reports. "I promised Mackenzie and Michaela I'd take them to see a movie."

"You're kidding!" I exclaim, leaning forward in my chair. "My kids won't be seen with me on a Friday night."

Kelly grins. "Poor Liz. It's obvious that I'm the 'cool mom.' "

"I hate to break it to you, Kel," says Jess, "but once Mackenzie and Michaela hit high school, you'll join us in the ranks of nerdy parents."

"Not me, girls. I've got a toe ring."

"That'll do it." Lucy laughs for the first time.

"I better get going too," says Mary Alice. "Craig has hockey tickets for the whole family, and the game starts at 7:00."

"You! At a hockey game!" howls Marina. "Have you ever watched a hockey game, Mary Alice? You'll be on the ice waving your first-aid kit before the end of the first period!"

"Don't worry. I've seen my share of rough-housing."

Marina snorts.

"You may be forgetting, Marina, that I was team mom when you coached Sally and Amy's soccer team. Some of those girls were brutal."

"How could I forget? You were the first parent referee to issue a red card to a player for bad manners. Trust me . . . you do not have the stomach for hockey!"

"OK, ladies, that's enough," Jess chimes in. "Marina, how about starting the car before you scare poor Mary Alice to death?"

"I hadn't realized how much I missed you guys," says Lucy as we begin to gather our things. "I hate to see you go."

"Is that an invitation to stay?" I tease.

"Could you? I mean, I'd love for you to stay, but I know you're busy, Liz. I don't want to interfere with your plans."

"What plans? John's on a fishing trip all weekend, and I'm a pariah to my kids on Friday night. I'll just tell them dinner is Yo-Yo."

I can tell by the circle of perplexed faces that my friends have no idea what I'm talking about. I explain that Yo-Yo in our home is shorthand for "you're on your own."

"Yo-Yo! I love it!" Marina gives me a high-five. "I don't have anything going on either, Luce. The twins are with their dad this weekend. And, as I said earlier, all of this talk about food has made me hungry. How about getting some dinner?"

I look at Lucy. "Sounds good to me."

"Sure," she agrees.

"Great! I'll just drop these social butterflies off while you escort Lucy to the shower and get her to change out of that pitiful flannel nightgown."

"Aye, aye, sir!" I tease, performing a mock salute.

"And I don't care where we go as long as they serve good pasta. I'm craving —"

"Marina, wait a minute," interrupts Lucy. "I'm really not feeling up to going out. I was thinking perhaps we could order something in."

"Too bad," Marina fires back. "You need to get out of this house. And if you put up a fuss, I'll ask some of my buddies at the station to stop by with lights and sirens. You wanna explain that to the neighbors, Luce?"

"Come on, Marina," Lucy pleads, turning to me for help. Finding none, she continues, "We can light a fire and have a cozy dinner right here —"

Marina cuts her off. "Number one: in its present shape, this place is not cozy. It's depressing. Number two: you need to wash your hair. I'll be back in twenty minutes.

You'd better be ready, Lucy, or I swear I'll call dispatch."

We settle on dinner at Drucillina's, a neighborhood restaurant known for fabulous homemade pasta and even better pizza. In celebration of Lucy's "coming out" party, I decide to put all concern of carbohydrates aside, reciting the perennial dieter's excuse: "I can always get back on my program tomorrow."

The proprietor, Drucillina's son, Clarenzo, stops by our table as we peruse the menu. *"Bella signorine!* It's so nice to see you," he exclaims in a thick Italian accent. "Signorina Lucy, I am so sorry to hear about your mama. She was a *molto speciale."*

"Thank you very much, Clarenzo. I know Mother was very fond of you and your restaurant."

"Thank you, signorina." He puts a fist to his heart and wipes a tear from his eye. "And where have you two been lately?" Clarenzo adds, turning to Marina and me. "You don't like my mama's ravioli no more?"

"Are you kidding? Everybody knows Mama Dru makes the best pasta this side of the Hill," replies Marina, referring to the

South St. Louis neighborhood of Italian immigrants where she grew up and her mother still resides.

"Then why I not see you?" he presses. "You no like my *ristorante?*"

"I'm afraid my diet's the culprit, Clarenzo," I interject. "I've been trying to watch my carb intake. But tonight I've decided to —"

"Carb?" he interrupts. "What's this you say? 'Carb'? You no like my *carbonara?*"

"No, no," I explain. "By carbs I mean food like bread and pasta. I'm trying to eat less of those things."

"What? You on a hunger strike?" He gestures wildly as people at other tables begin to look our way. "Signorina Lizzy, don't you know pasta is the food from God? The book of Exodus say the Good Lord himself ordered the semolina to come right down from the sky" — he wiggles his fingers like tiny raindrops — "to feed Moses and the Italians in the desert. You no believe in God, signorina?"

"Yes, I mean, no. Of course I believe in God." My eyes dart around the room, noticing the growing number of patrons who have taken more than a casual interest in the spectacle unfolding before them.

"Face it, Liz," Marina observes, "your lack

of carbohydrates is clouding your mind. How can you turn down the food God gave to the Italians in the desert? What were you thinking? Don't worry, Clarenzo, we're here to put an end to this nonsense."

"*Bene!* Then, I, Clarenzo" — he lifts his chin — "will make you *speciale* dinner tonight. Food to put some meat on your bones."

"*Grazie,* Clarenzo," says Marina, while I fervently pray that others in the restaurant have overheard Clarenzo's observation that I am in need of "some meat on my bones."

Our trek through Italian gastronomical paradise began as the waiter set a gorgeous antipasto platter before us, featuring succulent honeydew melon slices wrapped with paper-thin slices of prosciutto. The cool melon was the perfect mate for the spicy Italian bacon.

"How I've missed this place," says Lucy after her first luscious bite. "Judd and I used to come here all the time. He was such a tease. He and Clarenzo had this silly running joke."

"What was it?" I ask, catching a drop of juice that began to wander down my chin.

"Clarenzo would ask about our food, and Judd would respond that his dinner had 'too much oregano.' Clarenzo would toss his head back and hurl an insult in Italian, then they would both start laughing. I never could understand what was so funny. It's strange the things you remember." Tears glisten in her blue eyes.

At a loss for words, I examine the pattern of Clarenzo's silverware. As aggravating as John can be sometimes, I can't imagine being without him.

"I know what you mean." Marina spears another slice of melon. "Bobby and I considered Drucillina's 'our place.' It's where he took me on our first date. For a long time after the divorce, I couldn't even eat here — not that I didn't try. I wasn't about to let him take away my favorite restaurant too. But every time I tried to take a bite of food, I'd get a big knot in my throat. I couldn't help wondering if he'd taken 'her' here." Anger simmers in Marina's dark eyes.

"Oh, Rina," Lucy says. "I didn't mean to bring up any bad memories."

"Don't worry about it, Luce. I'm fine with it now. That's not to say I didn't wallow in bitterness for a while. In fact, I relished it! I did my best to hide it from the twins, but Kimmie could always see through me."

"Alli calls every day." Lucy shakes her head. "I know she's checking up on me. I've tried to convince her that everything's fine, but I can tell she doesn't believe me."

I finally find my voice. "But, Lucy, you are far from fine. Alli's your daughter. She loves you. She deserves to know that you're struggling. And besides, you are all she has left."

"And what a prize I am!" Lucy surprises me with her angry tone. "The poor girl loses her wonderful dad and beloved grandmother, and all she has left is a mother who can't even sleep in her own bedroom."

"Preach it, sister!" Marina gives a sardonic laugh. "I've been there. I remember thinking, 'What kind of mother am I if even my cheating rat of a husband rejected me?'"

"Come on, Marina," I begin.

Her eyes grow thoughtful. "No, it's true, Liz. I was so full of anger that I wasn't even sure who I was mad at from day to day. One day I'd be ranting about the hussy who seduced my husband. The next day I'd convince myself that Bobby was a world-class jerk and I was better off without him. Then, before I knew it, I was wondering what I did to chase him away. Was I too controlling? Not pretty enough? Did he feel neglected because of the twins? I could beat myself flatter than my mom pounds scaloppine."

"Marina, you're one of the most upbeat

people I know," I protest. "The last word I'd use to describe you is angry."

"I can put on a pretty good show when I want to. A lot has changed in the last few years."

"Such as? You're in the same house, same job . . . same nail salon," I tease in an effort to lighten the mood.

"Yes, I do have a killer nail technician." Marina laughs as she examines her meticulous manicure. "I guess the turning point for me was when a good friend told me that it's much easier to change *how* we react to a situation than to try to change the *situation*." She reaches for a crunchy breadstick and looks pointedly at Lucy. "This good friend also promised to pray for me. And she told me she would be there whenever I needed someone to talk to or a shoulder to cry on. This wise friend didn't wait for me to call her. She left little treats on my porch with encouraging notes and Bible verses. She'd stop by the precinct unannounced at noon and take me to lunch. This pushy friend even found out when I was having my nails done and made an appointment at the same time. That's when I realized I'd better give in, because I wasn't going to shake her."

Lucy's glistening eyes overflow with tears

under Marina's steady gaze.

I sit, stunned, and simply stare at Lucy across the table. "I didn't know," I say hoarsely. "You never said a word to the rest of us about how much Marina was struggling."

"My good friend understood how difficult it was for me to talk about the divorce," continues Marina. "Even though FAC was great, I was embarrassed. You all had your perfect little families, and mine was falling apart."

"Marina, you know we never judged you. The same thing could have happened to any of us." I swallow hard, thinking of all the times I haven't treated John as well as I should. I wince inwardly, feeling guilty for taking his presence and his care for me for granted. Suddenly I wish he were sitting next to me right now so I could give him a hug. But then again that sort of spontaneous female behavior might make him start to sweat . . .

Marina's quiet for a minute. Then she says slowly, "Liz, you are such a sweetheart. I know you say that now, and you may honestly mean it. But I also know that you can't imagine John ever cheating on you. Trust me, I never imagined it either. I thought Bobby and I had a good marriage. Sure, we had our arguments. And he could really be a slob." At this memory she laughs, then grows sober again. "But I loved him, and I'm pretty sure he loved me. I would've put the odds for me and Bobby breaking up at almost nil."

Marina stops talking. The silence at the table grows heavy.

She takes a breath. "But there I was . . . the only single mom on the block. And the women at PTA started clinging to their husbands' arms and giving me nasty glares, as if I were plotting to slip away with one of them to the janitor's closet."

"Marina!" I protest, horrified. "No one thought that! And if they did, they aren't worth a second thought."

"I know that now, Liz, and I guess I knew it down deep back then. But I felt so odd. Like I no longer belonged anywhere. It seemed like yesterday we were a couple, watching the twins play soccer. Then, all of a sudden, I was alone. It didn't seem fair."

"It wasn't fair," says Lucy quietly.

"I know, but that wasn't the point, as my friend told me during one particularly whiny lunch. This same wise friend explained that God sometimes allows trials in our lives to draw us closer to Him and to prepare us for future challenges. She also said that, just like athletes, we can't build strength without a little strain."

Lucy looked away as the waiters cleared the antipasto and placed a fresh tomato salad before each one of us. I knew from experience that Drucillina had likely plucked the ripe tomatoes and fragrant basil leaves from her garden. She then drizzled the luscious concoction with olive oil to make a simple but mouth-watering salad. I couldn't wait to dig in.

"Has anyone noticed that, so far, this meal is extremely low carb?" I marvel at the burst of flavor that passes over my tongue.

Marina rolls her eyes. "Let go of the guilt, Liz. Just enjoy your dinner."

"I'll stop the diet talk if you finish your story."

"Well, I'd like to say that my eyes were opened at lunch by Lucy's sage advice — and everyone lived happily ever after. But you already know I'm much too pigheaded for that. Instead I told my dear friend that I didn't need any more challenges and that I certainly wasn't in the mood to talk about God. 'Fine,' my friend said sweetly. 'Then keep doing things your way.' That comment shut me up — and frankly put a bit of a damper on our lunch. By the time I checked back in at the precinct, I'd decided to put in a request to change my lunch hour so next time I'd have an excuse to ditch Lucy if she happened to stop by with another piece of helpful advice."

Lucy smiles. "I never knew that, Marina. A little passive-aggressive, hmm?"

Marina grins back. "I guess I deserve that. But can I at least finish my story before you make me stretch out on the analyst's couch?"

"Go on, Marina," I say, shushing Lucy.

"When I climbed in my car after the shift, I noticed a slip of paper fluttering under the wiper. I snatched it off the windshield and saw Lucy's handwriting. My first thought was to crumple it up. But thinking it might be an apology for her insensitive comments, I decided to read what she'd written. It wasn't an apology or a note. It was simply a Bible verse: 'You use steel to sharpen steel, and one friend sharpens another. Proverbs 27:17.' "

Marina's voice catches, and she takes a sip of water before continuing. "Well, that did it. The floodgate opened. I sat in that car on what had to be the hottest day in July and cried my eyes out. I knew how hard it had been for Lucy to confront me. Hey, I know how hard it is for *anyone* to confront me. I *train* to be scary. Maybe I even scared

Bobby off, who knows? So I decided the least I could do was give Lucy's way — God's way — a chance."

"Marina . . . ," says Lucy.

"Luce, I bet you didn't know I kept all of your notes in my bag, did you? They were kind of a security blanket for the times I felt all alone. I needed to know that someone who wasn't related to me cared. I mean, I'm close to my family, but they *have* to love me. It's required. At least that's what my mom always pounded into us."

I see Marina swallow hard. She had so rarely talked about her divorce or her ex-husband at FAC, and now I know why.

"But a friend has a choice," Marina adds. "Just knowing that you had chosen to love me . . . for *me* . . . helped me crawl out of bed on some really dark days."

"I had no idea." I feel like an insensitive fool.

"Marina, you are too hard on yourself," says Lucy. "You are such a strong —"

"Will you please let me finish before I start bawling in my salad?"

Lucy nods. My throat is too tight for words.

"Anyway, I pulled your notes out of my bag — and dug my dusty Bible from the glove compartment. I began to read the very first card you gave me. I remember it because it was the one attached to that jar of starter for Amish Friendship Bread that I was supposed to stir every day for three weeks or something like that. By the way, what made you think I would ever make that bread?"

Lucy smirks. "I should have known better. I bet you threw it out, didn't you?"

"Of course I threw it out. Who in their right mind would do all that work just to make a loaf of bread?"

"You actually threw it out?" I ask. "I've felt guilty for years, thinking I broke some bond of friendship by not making that bread."

Marina snorts. "Lizzy, get a life! Do you want to hear the end of my story or not?"

"Go on," I answer sheepishly.

"Anyway, Lucy's card referred to Jeremiah 29:11. I looked the verse up in my Bible and read it over and over. I wanted to make sure I'd read it right. It said, ' "For I know the plans I have for you," declares the LORD, "plans to prosper you and not to harm you, plans to give you hope and a future." ' I remember thinking, *Could this be true? Does God really have plans to* prosper *me? Do I really have hope for the future?* This may seem simplistic, but to someone who was looking for an excuse each morning to pull the covers back over her head, it was an epiphany. I thought about that verse all the way home." Marina wiped tears from her eyes. "For the first time since Bobby left, I didn't feel alone."

"Rina, I told you I was there for you," says Lucy.

"Luce, please don't take this the wrong way. I treasure your friendship and support. But at that time, I needed something more than you could give me. I didn't know it then, but what I really needed was to reconnect with God."

Marina stares at the table. "You both know I was a believer. I knew Jesus paid for my sins on the cross, and because of this someday I'd see Him face to face in heaven. But right then I needed to get through the next day. Waiting for heaven just seemed too far away. Until I opened my Bible that afternoon and allowed God to speak to me through His Word, I thought He'd forgotten about me. Or, worse, that He didn't care."

Marina lifts her head, and I see a renewed determination in her eyes. " 'For I know the plans I have for you . . .' Ladies, those words woke a longing in me I didn't even know was there. That night I looked up all the verses you had given me, Lucy, and underlined them in my Bible. I've clung to those promises more times than Liz has cheated on her diet."

"Hey!" I toss a breadstick at Marina.

"What are you worrying about?" she teases. "Clarenzo thinks you need to be fattened up."

As if on cue, a team of waiters emerges from the kitchen with the main course Clarenzo had prepared *speciale* for us. A steaming platter of *brasciole* — a traditional Italian meat roll simmered to perfection and covered with a hearty red sauce — is accompanied by a generous bowl of tiny homemade gnocchi, laced with savory roasted garlic butter and Romano cheese.

"Now this . . . this is food!" cries Clarenzo as the plates pass before our wide eyes on the way to the table. *"Mangia, signorine! Mangia!"*

And *mangia* — "eat" — we do. Not wanting to insult Clarenzo, I finish every morsel of food set before me, even using the crusty Italian bread to scoop up the last bit of sauce from my plate.

I'm so full I can barely move. What was I thinking?

Before I have time to answer this question, the cappuccino comes. As I sip the warm drink from a tiny cup, I'm paying the price for my gluttony.

I moan. "I hope Clarenzo isn't planning on closing early, because there's no way I can walk to the car right now."

"Me neither." Lucy's eyes are closed, and her head is resting on the back of the booth.

"Wimps," says Marina, even though I can detect a bit of grogginess in her voice too. "My mom cooks like this every day."

"Then you have one high metabolism, sweetheart," I observe, pointing toward Marina's trim physique. "And, by the way, have I told you lately that I hate you?"

No one at the table has the energy to respond.

"Signorine," announces Clarenzo, jarring me from my snooze, "to complete your meal — *dolce!* You like chocolate, no?"

Before we could protest, Clarenzo places a huge piece of Drucillina's signature dessert, Death by Chocolate, on the table. "Since you on a diet, Signorina Lizzie, I bring one piece and three forks."

"Thank you, Clarenzo," I manage to say, convinced that tonight the dessert may just live up to its name.

Even though the three of us are so full we were barely able to waddle out to Marina's car, Lucy seems to be feeling better as we pull into her driveway after dinner. Maybe it *is* all the chocolate — the "miracle food" — I theorize.

"So admit it," teases Marina as Lucy gets out of the car. "Wasn't this worth missing a movie on the Lifetime channel?"

"Come on," I hiss, "give her a break."

"No, that's OK, Liz," says Lucy. "I hate to admit it, but you're right. I needed to get out of the house." She cocks her head toward Marina and grins. "And I definitely wouldn't have done so without your bullying."

"Me? A bully? You know I'm a pussycat, Luce!"

Lucy just laughs.

"Maybe of the man-eating variety," I add under my breath as we drive away.

■ ■ ■ ■

CHAPTER FIVE

■ ■ ■ ■

MOM'S LAUNDRY SECRETS

Add one cup of white vinegar to the rinse
cycle to dissolve alkaline residue to leave
clothes soft and sweet smelling.

Blot antiperspirant stains with a solution
of white vinegar and baking soda. Wash
as usual.

Loosen dried-on glue by soaking a clean
cloth in white vinegar and saturating the
spot until it's gone.

Apply a mixture of one part white vinegar
and two parts water to grass stains, and
blot. Repeat as needed and wash as
usual.

Dab white vinegar on mildew and let item
sit in the sun. Wash separately.

Harris Fun Night Gorp

1 cup M&M candies
1 cup salted nuts
1 cup dried cranberries
8 cups unbuttered popcorn, popped

Instructions

1. Mix together in a large bowl.
2. Enjoy!

A few minutes later, I walk into my home to find Daisy sleeping peacefully on a pile of clean laundry that one of my family members obviously took from the dryer and dumped on a chair. Naturally it would not occur to any member of the family to fold this laundry or, heaven forbid, put it away. After all, that's Mom's job.

I have no idea who started this vicious rumor, but it's a widely held belief that the meticulous care of each family member's wardrobe is my responsibility. Frankly, I have done all I can to dispel this falsehood: from assigning each child a designated day on which to wash his or her own clothing to demonstrating my complete ineptitude in this area. How many shrunken sweaters and bleach-speckled shorts will it take to convince my family that laundry is not one of my core competencies?

It's not just that I'm "domestically challenged" in the area of laundry. I actually *loathe* it. I'm not sure why. I wasn't raised to view this domestic necessity as an undue burden. In fact, my mother still gets absolutely giddy about the prospect of turning a huge pile of dirty clothes into neatly folded and color-coded stacks ready to slide into waiting drawers.

I'll never forget the time she came to help

after I had Hannah . . .

"Liz, let me help you," Mom cooed as I complained about the mountain of dirty clothes in my laundry room. "I love to do laundry!"

"Mom, you have to be kidding. What in the world is there to 'love' about doing laundry?"

"Oh, I don't know," she replied, expertly pouring fabric softener into an orifice I didn't even know existed in my washing machine. "It's just nice to have everything all clean and fresh."

I rolled my eyes. "Mom, mark my words. Those clothes will be dirty, smelly rags by sunset, and we'll be right back where we started. It's like a bad horror movie, and I'm the empty-headed victim who keeps falling for the plot of the evil mastermind."

"Liz, you've always had such a sense of humor!" she said.

Actually, I wasn't trying to be funny. But I also wasn't about to argue when she began to sort socks . . .

I pull my mind back to the present and shoo Daisy off the pile of clean clothing. I sniff a couple of the T-shirts on top. They have a definite dog smell. *Do I toss these back in the dirty laundry pile? Or should I just put them away and hope Josh doesn't get a whiff of our wily Westie?* Once again I'm faced with every mother's dilemma when making such a choice: would I be able to hold up under the questioning of Dr. Phil?

I picture myself in the good doctor's hot seat before a TV audience of six million "good mothers" . . .

A tearful Josh has just explained to the empathetic Dr. Phil that his mother expects him to wear clothing from the dog's bed.

"Could this be true, Mrs. Harris?" asks Dr. Phil.

I'm not sure if I've heard his question correctly since I've been focusing on holding in my stomach and clenching my thighs in an effort to present a slimmer silhouette before the cameras, which seem to be filming me from every conceivable angle. I'm also trying to jut out my chin because I've heard this will disguise the wrinkles on my neck and make me appear more confident. With all this on my mind, I've completely lost track of the conversation.

"Mrs. Harris . . . Liz . . . do you realize that this sort of behavior is considered child abuse in many states?" Dr. Phil persists.

"No, no, no, I would never abuse my

children," I protest. "It's just that the kids never fold the laundry from the dryer. Then it ends up —"

"Are you saying that you think the proper parental response to this childish misstep is to force your young son to wear the flea-infested clothing from the bed of a dog?" . . .

As the image of Dr. Phil recedes in my mind, I sigh. Once again convinced I'll never be a match for the good doctor, I gather the clothes from the chair and walk through the kitchen to the laundry room.

As I fill the washer, I wonder, *Where does all this laundry come from anyway?* My children constantly tell me they have no clean clothes. If that's the case, whose clothes make up the four loads I do each day?

And what happens to all the towels I wash every week? I sometimes wonder if an evil little creature lives in the corner of the linen closet, just waiting to devour my clean bath towels as soon as I stack them on the shelf, leaving me only a few thin washcloths to dry my shivering frame after a shower.

I consider exploring this subject further in one of my weekly columns. One of the perks of writing a lifestyle column in the local newspaper is having access to a number of domestic divas anxious to promote their products and services. Perhaps one of these experts will turn out to be a true maven in the laundry room — providing a series of tips to transform this daily drudgery into a delight.

Fat chance.

I will never be my mother.

While I sit at the kitchen table, waiting for the washer to finish the spin cycle, I notice a strange light flickering under the basement door. I'd thought I was alone in the house, so I quickly tick off the whereabouts of family members on my fingers.

Let's see. John is on a fishing trip until tomorrow night.

Hannah is sleeping over at her best friend, Kimberly's, house — promising she'll be in bed at a reasonable hour. Yeah, right.

I look at my watch and notice it's only 10:30 — too early for my teens to be home on a Friday night. I've learned from parents who have emerged from their children's teenage years with their sanity intact that most teens view coming home even a minute before curfew as too "geeky" for words.

So, where could the light be coming from? *Perhaps an intruder slipped into the house while I've been tending to domestic duties,* I theorize. I always suspected there was something unsafe about laundry!

I gently press my ear to the basement door. Hearing nothing, I open the door a crack and peer down the stairs. The light is definitely coming from the rec room — casting multicolored shadows like some overenergized disco ball.

So what do I do now? Do I creep down the stairs, armed with an umbrella like some dimwit in a suspense film?

Wait a minute. Where's our fearless Westie?

Of course, Daisy, who leaps at the door in a raucous frenzy at the sight of the UPS man, is nowhere to be found. Figures. She's probably still sleeping off all that cinnamon toothpaste from this morning.

I could call John on his cell phone. He and his fishing buddies should be in from the lake by now. But before I punch the first number on the handset, I change my mind, remembering the last time I called him on one of these weekends of "male bonding" . . .

"John? We have an emergency!" I whispered frantically into the phone.

"Liz? Is that you? I can barely hear you."

"I can't speak any louder. I don't want to startle it."

"What do you mean 'it'? What don't you want to startle? Liz, are you all —"

"No, I am *not* all right," I interrupted. "John, I don't know what to do. There's a mouse in the kitchen light fixture!"

"A what?" There was a pause, and then he began to laugh. "Did you say a mouse?"

"John, please! This is serious. Katie and Hannah are locked in their rooms, and I don't know what to do. You know how scared I am of mice. You have to come home."

Another pause. "Liz, I can't leave now. Just ask Josh to —"

"Josh is already gone," I said even more frantically. "He's working as a referee at the soccer tournament this weekend. He won't be home for hours."

"Then just wait until he —"

"John, I *can't* wait! The girls are locked in their rooms, and I cannot live in a house with a mouse running around in the ceiling. You have to come home."

"Liz, I am not coming home. It's a three-hour drive," he said in his most reasonable voice. "Now listen, all you need to do is —"

I cut him off. "I am *so not* touching a rodent, John!"

"Calm down, sweetheart," he said over what sounded like laughing in the background. "Remember, you're the adult here."

"An adult who would rather give up her favorite sweatpants than come face to face with that beady-eyed rodent," I whined. "You should see its long, skinny tail flipping around up there. John, I just can't —"

"Liz, listen." The amusement had begun to fade from his voice. "You don't have to touch the mouse. Just put a trash bag over the light fixture and tap the glass. The mouse will run right into the bag."

"What if it chews its way out of the bag and gets away?" I asked warily. "Mice carry a virus."

"Liz, you have two choices," he insisted as my hopes for a valiant rescue began to fade. "You are going to have to handle this yourself . . . or wait until I get home. *Tomorrow.*"

"But —"

"And don't even think about staying at a hotel."

It always annoys me when John knows what I'm thinking. Sometimes even before I think it.

After much discussion and two trips to Wal-Mart, the girls and I ended up catching the mouse in a live trap baited with a peanut-butter-smeared cracker. By the time we were ready to release the well-fed critter in the park, Hannah had named him Pinky . . .

No, it's probably not a good idea to call John. Especially since he's fishing with the same group of guys from our small group at church. I am still periodically asked, "Seen any killer mice lately, Liz?" by snickering males. Since we are usually in church at the time, I just smile. But all the while, I'm really thinking that I'd like to see how these macho men would stand up under a leg waxing.

My options are narrowing. Maybe I should call Marina. No, I'd never forgive myself if she were injured in the line of duty by what I've now convinced myself is a crazed assassin in the basement. I'll just have to handle this myself.

After arming myself with the meat mallet from my kitchen utensil drawer, I take a deep breath and start down the stairs.

"Josh? Katie? Are you there?" I call, trying to sound casual. "I just wanted you to know that your DAD and I are home. And Marina — the POLICE OFFICER next door — is here too. We're going to watch a movie before she goes on her shift. By the way, she has her GUN with her, so don't make any quick moves. Ha, ha. Right, Marina?"

Even I am embarrassed by my inane babbling. I bet I have the serial killer in the basement just shaking in his boots.

Before I can plot another plan of attack, the door of the rec room bursts open. Startled, I drop the meat mallet on my foot . . . and slide down the last three stairs. I land solidly on my tailbone.

"Mom?" It's the voice of my oldest child. "What's —"

Still immersed in the world of true crime, I whisper hoarsely, "Katie! Run!"

"Mom, what's wrong? And what are you doing with this?" She bends over and picks up the meat mallet.

I drift back to reality as Katie helps me up from the floor. I realize there is no mass murderer in the basement. And the mysterious light? It's coming from the television.

"What are you doing home so early?" I ask my daughter. "I thought you went to a movie with Kristin."

"I had a change of plans. Kim got sick, so her mom had to cancel the sleepover. Hannah looked so crushed that Josh and I decided to change our plans and stay home with her. We're having a fun night."

A "fun night" is a tradition I thought my

teens had long outgrown. In years past they would convince us to rent a movie and — if we were feeling especially generous — a video game. Then they'd load up on junk food and settle in the rec room with plans to stay up to see the sunrise. John and I could never quite grasp the "fun" in this sort of night. Our idea of fun is sinking into our pillow-topped mattress, pulling up the cozy down comforter, and settling in for a "long winter's nap."

"So Josh and Hannah are here too?" I ask.

"Yeah, they're asleep in front of the television. I guess I conked out too. Hannah wanted to watch *The Little Princess* again. I usually nod off after Miss Minchin forces Sarah to live in the attic."

I peek in the door of the rec room. The scene transports me back in time. There are three sleeping bags and pillows lined up on the floor. Various bags of chips, a bowl of gorp, and several cans of pop litter the adjacent coffee table.

My tall, lanky son is stretched out on the floor next to his little sister. His hand loosely circles a pop can. Hannah's head is snuggled into her favorite stuffed dog that she calls Eddie Jr. I can still see the imprint of Katie's body on the sleeping bag next to Hannah, indicating that she, too, joined her brother and sister on the floor so as not to break a fun-night tradition.

My state of high anxiety melts into sweet serenity. There is no sight more precious to a mother than watching her children sleep. But even more precious on a day that started out so badly is a glimpse of the genuine bond between these often contentious siblings. Despite their bickering, this scene reminds me that they do truly love each other. Although they may not realize it, I know the ties they are forging will give them strength now — and into adulthood.

Yes, God knew what He was doing when He formed the family.

Forcing myself to turn from the heart-warming sight before me, I take my meat mallet from a still-confused Katie, give her a quick hug, and whisper, "Have fun, sweetie."

And then I tiptoe up the stairs . . . so as not to disturb my children and break the spell.

■ ■ ■ ■

CHAPTER SIX

■ ■ ■ ■

Blue Plate Special at Sally's Diner
Sally's Meat Loaf

1 1/2 lbs. very lean hamburger
1 egg
1 cup fresh breadcrumbs
1/2 cup onion, chopped
1/2 cup carrot, shredded
1 teaspoon dried sage (leaf, not ground)
1/2 teaspoon salt
1/4 teaspoon pepper
1 clove of garlic, minced
Dash of Worcestershire sauce
1/2 cup ketchup

Instructions

1. Mix all ingredients and shape into a loaf.
2. Bake at 350 degrees for 1 hour.
3. Drain off fat, if necessary, and bake for 5–10 more minutes.

4. Remove from oven and let stand for 10 minutes before slicing.
5. Serve with brown gravy or ketchup.

"Real" Mashed Potatoes

2 1/2 pounds Yukon or russet potatoes, cut into 1-inch chunks (about 7–8 cups)
1/3 cup milk or half-and-half
1/4 cup butter
Salt and pepper to taste

Instructions

1. Place potatoes in a 4-quart pan, cover with water, and bring to a boil.
2. Reduce heat and simmer for 20 minutes, or until potatoes are tender.
3. Drain water. Add remaining ingredients and beat by hand or with electric mixer until light and creamy.

Country String Beans

1 lb. fresh green beans
1 oz. salt pork or bacon
1 teaspoon salt

Instructions

1. Wash beans. Remove the strings and snap off ends.
2. Cook beans and salt pork/bacon in an uncovered pot for 1–2 hours.
3. Add salt the last half hour of cooking.

MILE HIGH COCONUT CREAM PIE

1 (6 oz.) box coconut pudding or pie filling mix
1 cup fresh coconut, coarsely shredded
1 baked 9-inch pie shell (deep dish)
6 cups fresh, sweetened whipped cream

Instructions

1. Prepare pudding as directed on package. Cool.
2. Add half the coconut to cooled pie filling. Pour into pie shell; chill.
3. Spread whipped cream over pie, mounding in center.
4. Toast remaining coconut in oven at 400 degrees for 2–3 minutes. Sprinkle over pie when cool.

Before going to bed (minus the meat mallet) on Friday night, I had picked up a message on my voice mail from Kelly, asking me to meet her at Lucy's at 8:15 the next morning.

This morning, as I hit the snooze alarm again, I muse, *Why me? I mean, I love Lucy, but how come I always end up as sidekick to my strong-willed friends whenever there's a sticky situation? Why not call Jess? She's the "wise" one. Or Marina? She has the guts to say what she thinks. And although she might not say much, Mary Alice would at least bring treats.*

I hate to admit it, but I suspect I end up in this role because I represent the path of least resistance. I can easily imagine Kelly's carefully plotted rationale for asking me to be a part of this little powwow.

Number one: she has already decided what Lucy needs to do to resolve her current problems and sketched out a plan of action.

Two: she believes it will be easier to convince Lucy that she's right if another member of FAC backs her up.

And three: she's confident I don't have the nerve to disagree with what she "knows" is best for Lucy.

What's hard for me to face is that Kelly's

probably right. I'm one of those people who clings to the hope that if I ignore a problem long enough, it will just work itself out. So far, what my husband calls my "theory of positive procrastination" has little to support its veracity. Unfortunately, my inaction has also resulted in more than a few personal and family crises. Ones that I'd rather not rehash.

Unwilling to delve any deeper into these murky emotional waters — and knowing it will be hours before the kids wake up from their fun night — I roll out of bed and drag myself to the shower.

Before I leave for Lucy's, I write the kids a note, just in case. But I figure I'll be back well before they roll out of their sleeping bags . . . just in time for lunch.

After only a couple of hours at Lucy's house, I'm feeling even more exhausted. Kelly has transferred Lucy's decision-making process to 4×6-inch cards, with the pros and cons listed neatly in columns.

"See? Isn't this easier when it's all on paper?" she asks, shuffling through the stack. "Where should we start?"

"How about next week?" answers a glazed-eyed Lucy. "I'm too tired to deal with this now, Kel."

Amen, sister, I'm thinking as I slouch on the couch.

"No problem." Kelly seems unruffled. "I'm flexible. Let's take a break. How about lunch?"

"In case you haven't noticed in your whirl of efficiency, it's only 10:30," I say. "I think we need a distraction . . . something fun."

"OK," concedes Kelly. "What do you have in mind?"

"A nap?" Lucy suggests.

Kelly flashes her a stern look. "Not an option."

"Pedicure?" I suggest.

"It's Saturday, and the nail salon will be jammed," Kelly reasons, straightening the index cards into a neat pile. "We'll never get three chairs together without an appointment."

"You're right," I admit. "I hate trying to talk across someone I don't know."

"Wait! I have an idea!" Kelly slips the cards into a lime green pocket folder. "Why don't we drive down to your aunt's home in Tredway to take a look at the house?"

"Oh no, no." Lucy shakes her head. "Not today. I thought we were going to wait and plan an FAC down there . . . when everyone can come along."

"Actually, Lucy, I think your first visit

116

would be easier with just me and Liz," says Kelly. Catching my annoyed look from the corner of her eye, she continues, "There will be less commotion this way. We'll have plenty of opportunities for all of us to see the house and meet your aunt."

"Well, we just can't pop in on her," insists Lucy, her voice rising. "I'd need to call first."

Kelly shrugs. "So call."

"I can't just call and say we'll be there in an hour!" Lucy exclaims. "I need to give her some notice . . . make sure she'll be home."

"Get real, Lucy." Kelly is already packing up her bag. "She's ninety-some years old and, if she's anything like Jess's grandma, probably driving a golf cart. I doubt she'll be hard to find."

The hour drive to Tredway is a true test of friendship.

Even though Lucy couldn't reach her aunt by phone, Kelly convinced us to go anyway. She also insisted on driving.

Before we left I called to check on the kids and make sure Josh or Katie would be home to keep an eye on Hannah until I returned that afternoon. After assuring them my cell phone would be on if they needed to get in touch with me, I strapped myself in the back seat of Kelly's car to prepare for what I knew would be a wild ride.

Kelly is one of those strong-willed women who drives just like she makes decisions — fast and with no regrets. As I grip the armrest, I realize that her driving style resembles that of my older daughter, Katie. Remembering a number of terrifying rides as Katie's passenger, I begin to break out in a cold sweat . . .

From the moment Katie poked her head into the world, she had a will of iron — even refusing to breathe for what my husband still calls the longest minute of his life. When our stubborn newborn finally agreed to take her first breath, the obviously rattled doctor examined her and informed us that nothing appeared to be wrong. He said she had just decided to begin breathing in her own time. Then he added cryptically, "Just wait until the teen years."

Little did we know how prophetic his words were. Shortly after Katie acquired her driver's license, she shared her belief that the majority of drivers on the road were inept. In fact, after completing the driver's exam, she didn't hesitate to express concern about the qualifications and abilities of her examiner.

"Where do they get these people?" she exclaimed as we walked from the licensing bureau. "She took points off my score for driving 29 in a 25-mph zone."

"Katie, 25 is the speed limit on residential streets," I said, appropriately proud of my familiarity with the *Nebraska Driver's Manual.*

"Mom, *nobody* drives 25," she replied sagely — another example to bolster her belief that parents are clueless.

I explained that this was the law, intended to make the roads safe for her and other drivers. I also informed my daughter that she would not have access to the family car until agreeing to follow the traffic laws — including speed limits.

I was able to secure her promise to adhere to the rules of the road, including the laws she considered pointless. However, she couldn't help adding that, in her opinion, anyone over thirty should be required to retake the driving test each year.

It was a good thing I clamped my lips shut, because my reply would not have been pretty . . .

This morning, as I watch the countryside fly by in blazing autumn colors on the curvy roads to Tredway, I realize I am not in the car with an appropriately cautious middle-aged driver. No, I'm experiencing an unwelcome glimpse of "Katie Gone Wild."

"Hey, Kelly," I say finally. "I'm feeling a little woozy back here. Would you mind slowing down a little?"

"Just keep your eyes on the horizon. You'll be fine."

I shut my eyes and pray that Tredway will be around the next hairpin curve.

When we reach Tredway, our first order of business is to find Aunt Bette.

"I'm still uncomfortable just dropping in," says Lucy after another unsuccessful try to reach her aunt by phone. "She's always been very gracious, but it doesn't seem right just showing up on her doorstep after all these years. She probably won't even recognize me."

"Don't worry, Lucy," I tease. "You've hardly changed from high school. In fact, isn't that the twin set you wore for your senior picture?"

"Very funny, Farrah." Lucy laughs, referring to my futile efforts to mimic the hairstyle of the popular Charlie's Angel during my younger days.

I probably deserved Lucy's teasing. After

all, it had been my idea, five years ago, to invite our FAC group to an old-fashioned slumber party — complete with sleeping bags, manicures, chick flicks, and an over-abundance of chocolate. On a whim I'd asked them to bring along their high-school yearbooks so we could see what each other looked like B.K. — before kids. The slumber party has become an annual FAC tradition, but instead of sleeping bags in my den, we now treat ourselves to an overnight at a hotel.

"What's the address again, Lucy?" asks Kelly.

"I don't have the address with me, but I know it's on Locust. I remember it being up on a hill."

"Why don't we stop and ask directions?" I suggest. "Your aunt has lived here all her life. I'm sure someone will know the house."

"No need. I can find it," Kelly insists.

I've learned from experience that it's not worth arguing with Kelly when it comes to directions — or just about anything else.

We circle the town square twice with no luck locating Locust Street. Since we drove into town from the north, Kelly decides to look for Locust south of the tiny downtown area. No luck.

Heading back into town after that futile

search, I again broach the subject of asking for directions. After all, my queasy stomach could use even a short break.

"Liz, I have an inborn directional ability." Kelly makes a sharp right on a road leading east of town.

Lucy and I are silent as the scenery changes from houses to a soybean field.

When the asphalt road switches to gravel, I see Kelly's jaw tighten as she slams on the brakes and makes a U-turn in the middle of the road. Gravel spits from under the tires as we roar west.

"Kelly, you might want to be careful," Lucy says softly. "Sometimes these small towns have speed traps."

An instant later a flashing red light fills the car's rear window.

"Great!" Kelly moans. "This is all I need! I just finished court diversion for my last ticket. David will never let me hear the end of this." She pulls to the shoulder of the two-lane county road.

It must be the luck of the Irish! I can't believe Kelly is able to charm her way out of a speeding ticket. As soon as she reads the cop's nametag — Callahan — our fearless leader flashes an impish grin and dives feet first into the role of "a simple Irish lass

grateful for the help of the kindly constable."
I will not be surprised if she slips into an
Irish brogue.

"Officer, thank heaven you found us!"
Kelly says before the elderly cop can even
ask for her driver's license and vehicle
registration. "We're here to visit my friend's
dear aunt, Miss Henrietta Crawford. And
silly me, I forgot the directions. I'm afraid
we're hopelessly lost. You wouldn't know
Miss Crawford, by any chance, would you?"

The helpful officer does indeed know
Aunt Bette. In fact, he informs us that just
yesterday she had moved from her home —
fondly referred to as Locust Hill — to new
quarters in nearby Orrick.

"I saw Janelle up at the house 'bout an
hour ago," says Officer Callahan.

"Did you say Janelle, Officer?" Lucy leans
across the front seat to look out the driver's
side window. "Is Janelle still with Aunt
Bette?"

My journalistic instincts kick in. *Who's
Janelle? Lucy hasn't said anything about a
Janelle.*

But now isn't the time to ask questions.

"Yep, ever since she was a teenager," says
the officer. "I 'spect she's up there doin'
some last minute straightenin' up. I'm sure
she wouldn't mind if you ladies looked

123

around."

In the end we don't need directions to Aunt Bette's home. Instead, Kelly's Irish charm not only saves her from a speeding ticket but secures us a police escort to Locust Hill.

"I can't believe Aunt Bette has already moved," Lucy says as we walk up the long drive to the front porch. "She was always pretty independent, but I never imagined she'd try to move herself."

"Luce, she's lived here all her life," I reason. "I'm sure she had a friend or two in town who was willing to help. Like Janelle, for instance. Who is she anyway? Is she a relative?"

"I don't think so, but from what I remember, she and Aunt Bette seemed to be closer than some mothers and daughters I know. I once asked Mother about Janelle on our way home from a visit to Tredway. All she said was that she was a friend of the family — and then changed the subject. It almost seemed as if she was a little jealous of her relationship with Aunt Bette."

"I see that a lot when I'm counseling families," says Kelly, "when a neighbor or distant relative gets close to an older person who's living alone. The family is happy there's someone there to look out for the person, but they get a little miffed when a relationship develops."

"Kind of like that corny old song," I add. " 'Love is spelled t-i-m-e.' "

My friends groan.

"Anyway," I continue, sniffing imperiously, "if Aunt Bette and Janelle are still so close after all these years, I'm sure she helped with the move."

"Oh, yes, of course you're right, Liz. It just seems like so much for a woman at her age to organize — even with help."

"I think it's great," says Kelly as we climb the front steps. "Now I'm really looking forward to meeting this ninety-some-year-old who can move in the morning and serve tea in the afternoon."

When Lucy rings the bell, a large sturdy woman comes to the front door. She appears to be in her early sixties. A huge smile lights her dark face. "Well, I'll be," she says, opening the screen door. "This can't be our Lucy, can it?"

Lucy smiles sheepishly. "Yes, I'm afraid it's me, Janelle . . . although I feel a bit like a prodigal after all these years. I'm sorry for dropping in this way, but we . . . my friends and I . . . had hoped . . ."

"No need to apologize. I'm just tickled to

see you," she replies, opening the door wide and motioning us into the house. "Now come on in, and I'll fix us up with a pot of tea."

Entering the Locust Hill house is like stepping back in time. The first thing I notice is the quiet. Not just the kind of quiet devoid of dogs and kids, but the quiet only found in small towns. After retiring to a largely rural area, my mother-in-law once said she could actually hear the worms chewing on the tomatoes in her garden. And that's how Locust Hill feels: "chewing worm" quiet.

Janelle escorts us down the hall to a large and sunny kitchen. On one wall is a deep porcelain sink, surrounded by old-fashioned white-enameled cabinets with chrome handles and glass fronts. I wonder idly where a homemaker would stash her clutter when people came to visit. I suspect the glass fronts were retired after focus groups determined that women didn't really want visitors looking in their cupboards.

An enameled gas range, poised on four narrow legs, looks like it was ordered straight from a 1920s *Sears* catalogue. The pale green appliance has a small cooktop, elevated oven, and two drawers. The vintage refrigerator in the far corner of the room is short and stout, with its compressor perched on the top.

As I continue to survey the room, I notice that the kitchen is also devoid of the labor-saving appliances typically found in today's kitchens. Most noticeably absent are a dishwasher and microwave oven.

Although my mother didn't get her first Radar Range until I was out of high school, I hadn't realized how much I'd come to depend on the microwave until mine was broken a few years ago. Not only did being without this appliance take the "easy" out of Easy Mac, it brought a whole new meaning to thawing hamburger. I even had to look up a recipe for making popcorn on the stovetop.

And what did a family do before the advent of the dishwasher? I, unfortunately, am very familiar with the answer: "You wash, Liz, and I'll dry" was the common after-dinner refrain from my mother.

Today dishwashers are so common that advertisers have given up promoting the benefit of soap that guards against "dishpan hands." I bet today's young homemakers don't even know the meaning of "dishpan."

Lost in my thoughts as Janelle fusses with our tea, I begin to think this might be a good question for a TV show . . .

Picture dapper Regis of *Who Wants to Be a Millionaire?* asking a young woman, "So, Ashlee, now for the sixteen-thousand-dollar question. 'What is a dishpan?' Is it . . .

a. a derogatory term for teacher,
b. another name for bedpan,
c. a tray used to carry hot plates to the table, or
d. a container in which to wash dishes?"

Ashlee looks stumped. "I'm not familiar with this term, Regis."

"Well, you can always use one of your lifelines, Ashlee. Perhaps phone a friend — or take a chance by polling the audience."

"I think I will phone a friend, Reeg."

"Good choice. This audience looks a little shaky to me."

Nervous laughing from the audience.

Regis grins. "Hey! I call 'em like I see 'em."

More laughing.

"So, Ashlee," continues the jovial game-show host, "who would you like to call?"

"Well, it has to be someone up on today's hip language. I bet my sister's friend, Stacy, will know. Her daughter's in junior high . . ."

Waking from my daydream, I begin to panic at the thought of my icemaker going on the fritz. And then I smile at myself. I am so a product of the twenty-first century.

Just then the teakettle whistles. Within minutes Janelle joins us at the long kitchen table with our tea.

Lucy takes a sip of the steaming brew. "I hadn't realized how much I missed coming down to Locust Hill. I always meant to visit sooner and bring Alli, but time just seemed to fly by."

"Now, don't you go worryin' about that," Janelle soothes, smoothing her wiry black hair back into a bun. "Miss Henrietta knows you've been busy raisin' your family. Your momma used to tell us all about you and that grandbaby of hers."

"Mother loved being a grandmother." Lucy smiles sadly.

"That's for sure," agrees Janelle. "She was such a sweet thing. I was so sad to hear she passed on."

"I miss her very much." Tears brim on Lucy's lower lashes.

"I'm sure you do . . . 'specially after losin' your husband in that terrible plane wreck. Miss Henrietta put you on our prayer chain up at the church. I know she didn't let a day pass without prayin' for you herself."

"She did? Aunt Bette prayed for me?"

"Every day, like clockwork. She told me one time that she wondered what God was preparin' you for . . . seein' how you'd lost so much."

Lucy looked out the window, and I stared into my tea. Kelly broke the uncomfortable silence by asking Janelle how long she had known Aunt Bette.

"She and my mama were best friends since they were girls," says Janelle. "In fact, it was Miss Henrietta who set Mama up with my daddy."

"Really?" says Lucy. "I never knew that."

"How did they meet?" I ask.

"He was a young teacher over at the college where her daddy taught. Miss Henrietta thought he would be perfect for Mama. You know how girls are!"

"Aunt Bette as a matchmaker," muses Lucy. "I would have never guessed."

"Oh, she's a fox, that one." Janelle laughs. "I don't know how she finagled it, but she got both of 'em to dinner at Locust Hill. She knew it would be love at first sight, and she was right. Mama and Daddy got hitched just as soon as she graduated high school."

"That's a great story," says Kelly. "Your

Aunt Bette is a spunky old bird, isn't she, Lucy?"

"Apparently so. But, I have to admit, I don't remember this side of her."

"No, most folks only see her sweetness," Janelle points out. "And she's got plenty of that. When my mama died, I was only seventeen. Miss Henrietta took me in like her own daughter."

"You lived here at Locust Hill?" I ask.

"No, but I might as well have. I was here so much," Janelle explains. "Daddy was crushed, losing the love of his life. He kinda curled in on himself."

Lucy looks down and begins to run her fingernail back and forth through a gouge in the soft wood of the pine table.

"Miss Henrietta helped me through that time," continues Janelle, "even though I knew she was missin' Mama probably as much as I was. She even dug into that bag of tricks of hers and tried to fix me up with a boy at college, just like she did with Mama."

"You're kidding?" I ask. "Did it work?"

"Not this time. I found my William on my own. We've been married almost forty years now."

"I wonder if she tried to do the same thing with Mother," says Lucy.

"I wouldn't be surprised." Janelle chuckles. "Maybe that's why she didn't come around much 'til she was married."

"Did Mother visit Locust Hill often?" Lucy asks.

"Oh, goodness yes! She and Miss Henrietta would sit out there on the porch for hours . . . just talkin' and sippin' tea. After your grandma died, Aunt Bette was just about all the family your momma had left. 'Sides you and your daddy, that is."

"I hadn't realized Mother and Aunt Bette were so close. She rarely talked about her side of the family."

Janelle nods. "That's some people's ways. They keep things held in and don't talk about 'em. But don't worry, houses can talk. I think you'll find more 'n enough family history right here on Locust Hill."

With that cryptic comment, Janelle hands over a house key. "You take this, Lucy — I've got another one at my place. I'm 'bout done for today. You all just look around as long as you want and then close up."

After explaining the basic layout of the rooms, Janelle leaves us on our own to explore the old house.

"So, are you going to give us the grand tour, Lucy?" asks Kelly.

"I'm not sure how grand it will be, but let's go take a look."

Off the narrow foyer is what appears to be a small library on the right and a large parlor to the left. French doors at the far end of the parlor open to a formal dining room. Just past the steep set of stairs in the foyer is the kitchen. A four-season porch spans the rear of the house.

The floors and old-fashioned woodwork are softly polished walnut. Slight ripples are visible on the floorboards in the hall — a physical reminder of the generations who had walked there.

"Look at these floors!" I exclaim as we step into the parlor. "They're gorgeous."

"Not to mention the furniture." Kelly lifts a white protective cloth draped over a Victorian-style sofa. "I wonder why it's all covered up."

"I doubt Aunt Bette used these rooms very often," explains Lucy.

As we continue our tour of the old house, it's evident that Locust Hill has been well maintained, but that many of the rooms, especially on the second floor, appear not to have been used for years. As with the dining room and parlor, the antiques in the three bedrooms upstairs are covered.

Kelly and I chat in the hall as we wait for

Lucy to finish her inspection upstairs.

"I'm beginning to like this idea of covering furniture," I comment, peeking under a sheet draped over a small side table. "Just think, you'd never have to dust. Or, better yet, dig gummy bears from between the cushions."

"I had a friend whose mom had plastic slipcovers custom-made for all the upholstered furniture in the living room," adds Kelly. "I remember getting up from the sofa on a hot day and being mortified by the sweaty thigh prints I had left behind."

"You're kidding! You actually left an imprint?" I squeal with laughter.

"I sure did . . . but you can bet I never wore shorts to her house again."

Lucy emerges from one of the upstairs bedrooms and walks down the steep staircase to join us in the front hall. "Well, ladies, I think we've seen about all there is to see at Locust Hill. Are you ready to head back to Omaha?"

"I always seem to be the one bringing up food," I say, "but I'd like to get something to eat first. Is there a place in town where we can grab a bite?"

"There used to be a little café downtown, but I'm not sure if it's still open."

"Let's give it a shot. I'm hungry too,"

Kelly announces.

As Lucy digs for the key Janelle gave her in the pocket of her jacket, I notice an envelope tucked into the frame of a mirror next to the door. I move closer to read the old-fashioned script. "Lucy, this has your name on it."

"What?" She looks up.

"This letter." I remove the linen envelope from the frame. "It has your name written on it."

"Let me see." Kelly stands on tiptoe to peer over my shoulder. "Do you recognize the handwriting, Lucy?"

She examines the envelope. "Not really. I assume it's from Aunt Bette, but why would she leave a letter for me here rather than mailing it? I haven't been to Tredway for years. How could she know I would find this?"

"I wonder why Janelle didn't mention it," I say. "She had to notice the envelope when she was cleaning."

"Well, there's only one way to find out," Kelly insists. "Open it up."

"Not here." Lucy rubs her thumb over the writing on the envelope. "Let's get something to eat first. I think I'll need it."

We decide to stop for a late lunch at Sally's

135

Diner since it's the only restaurant in Tredway. Sally's is not the first restaurant where I've seen a blue plate special advertised, but it's the first place I've actually seen it served on a blue plate.

A sleepy-eyed waitress, probably in her late teens, hands us each a one-page laminated menu and says in a bored tone, "The special today is Sally's Meat Loaf." She is wearing a light pink smock with a frilly, scalloped collar. A large plastic daisy with "Kendra" printed in the center is pinned to her uniform. The silver stud in her pierced brow seems as out of place in small-town Nebraska as a Southern drawl in New York City.

"Do you know what you want yet?" asks Kendra, gazing out the window at something apparently more interesting than taking our order.

"Is the meat loaf any good?" I ask.

"I guess." Kendra drums her pencil on the order pad. "A lot of people order it."

"That's good enough for me," I say. "I'll have the special."

"Mashed or fried?" she asks.

"Mashed meat loaf?" I ask incredulously.

Kendra's eye roll reminds me a lot of Katie's. "Nooooo. Mashed *potatoes*. Would you like mashed potatoes or fried potatoes?"

"Oh, I'm sorry. Are they 'real' mashed potatoes . . . or instant?"

"What?" asks Kendra, clearly annoyed by my questions.

"Never mind. I'll have mashed potatoes."

"Beans or corn?"

"What kind —," I begin, then add quickly after noticing the look on the waitress's face, "forget it. Beans."

"Ranch or bleu cheese?"

I give her a blank stare.

"On your salad. Ranch or bleu cheese?"

"Sorry. Bleu cheese — on the side, please."

Kendra sighs and makes a note on her pad. Looking up, she points the eraser end of her pencil at Kelly.

"I'll have the same."

"Everything?" the waitress queries.

"Yep. How about you, Lucy? What are you having?"

"I'd like a small salad with —"

"Forget it. She'll have the special too," Kelly orders.

"But —," Lucy tries.

"No buts," interrupts Kelly. "Remember the FAC creed, 'Friends don't let friends eat dessert alone.' That goes for meat loaf too."

After cleaning our huge blue plates of every

morsel of Sally's scrumptious meat loaf —
and sharing a huge slice of homemade Mile
High Coconut Cream Pie — we waddle to
the car for the drive back to Omaha.

"I hope whoever created elastic was
awarded a Nobel Peace Prize," I say while
trying to devise a way to fasten my seat belt
with the seat reclined so I can sleep on the
way home. But considering Kelly's driving
record, I opt for safety and forgo my nap.

"Well, you've put it off long enough."
Kelly glances at Lucy through the rearview
mirror. "Don't you think it's time to find
out what's in your aunt's letter?"

"Maybe, but you both have to promise me
something first. I want your word that you
won't tell the rest of FAC what's in the letter until I decide to share it."

"Why?" I twist around to rest my chin on
the seat so I can see Lucy's face. "Do you
think it could be a confession? Maybe Aunt
Bette was a member of the mob? The grand
dame of the Soprano family . . . hiding out
in Tredway, Nebraska?"

"Very funny, Liz. It's just that I have a lot
to sort out, and I don't want to feel pressured into making any decisions. I love you
all, but you can be a bit opinionated at
times. This is something I need to work out
myself."

"Keeping secrets presents a clear journalistic dilemma for me," I announce. "But you've got us at a weak moment — strung out on comfort food. What do you think, Kel?"

"Don't worry, Lucy. We'll keep it to ourselves. Go ahead . . . read the letter."

Lucy takes the ivory envelope from the pocket of her coat, runs her fingernail under the flap, and extracts a single sheet of paper with "Henrietta Crawford" engraved across the top of the page. And then she reads aloud:

My dear Lucy,

Since you are reading this, I know you have been to Locust Hill, and that fact brings me immense delight. I left explicit instructions with Janelle, as well as my attorney, not to forward this note to you. I wanted you to find it yourself.

Why all this intrigue? Really, dear, no intrigue at all. I know you have been through a great deal of trauma in the past year and a half. The last thing I wanted to do was add another burden.

At the same time, I have been praying that you wouldn't make any rash decisions about the disposition of Locust Hill without first exploring the house's history. I knew if you felt strong enough to make the trip to Tredway, you would be strong enough to hear what I have to say.

My great-grandfather, Joseph Simmons, built Locust Hill in 1861. He, along with his wife and daughter, was one of the first settlers in Cramer County. Joseph was a man of strong faith who was not afraid to act on his principles. He served President Lincoln and the Union in the 46th Nebraska Cavalry during the war at great personal cost.

Joseph's wife, Emily, was also a person of strong convictions. She fought courageously, in her own way, for the values she shared with her husband — both before and after the war. As a woman living during the Victorian era, she did not receive any acknowledgment for much of her work.

Since it was built, direct descendants of Joseph and Emily have occupied Locust Hill. In fact, both your grandfather and I were born in the house. Its halls hold many fond memories.

For a time I left Tredway and Cramer County. When I returned to teach at the college, I accidentally came across some important information regarding our family history. Things that truly surprised me. That changed my views of our family . . . and perhaps the course of my own life. I will pass these documents along to you when you feel ready to read them. I think you'll find the information quite interesting.

For now, I ask that you indulge your old aunt and not make any hasty decisions regarding Locust Hill. Take some time to get to know the house. Although you may not understand it now, the history within its walls is part of you, and you are part of it. Please come see me when you are feeling up to it.

Much love,
Aunt Bette

"Is that it?" Kelly asks.

"Yes," replies Lucy, "except for her address and phone number at the retirement home. She is now living at Pacific Meadows over in Orrick, just as Officer Callahan told us."

Kelly's brow furrows in thought. "That means she must have written the letter recently . . . when she knew she'd be moving to Orrick."

"Her letter sounds a little mysterious," I say. "What do you think this important information about your family history might be?"

Lucy shrugs. "I have no idea, but I feel like I'm in the middle of an old episode of *Murder, She Wrote*."

"How can you say that, Lucy? We are decades younger than Jessica Fletcher!" exclaims Kelly. "Remember, dear, I have a toe ring!"

To ease Lucy's concern about Aunt Bette's cryptic letter, I promise to run a search of the newspaper's database to look for clippings about Locust Hill when I stop by the office on Monday. Thanks to the emergence of the Internet, a reporter can link to a host of online libraries as well as the files of newspapers around the country. It never ceases to amaze me what typing in a few keywords and a couple of clicks of the mouse can bring up on my computer screen.

"Liz, you are so sweet." Lucy gives me a quick hug.

We are standing in Lucy's driveway as Kelly roars down the street — finally free to cruise without my white-knuckled comments from the next seat. Maybe I should offer to drive next time.

"No problem," I say. "I'm happy to do it. You know I love a good mystery. But I have to warn you, we'll probably be disappointed. These articles are usually pretty dry . . . like they were written by a Joe Friday wannabe. 'Just the facts, ma'am.' "

"As far as I'm concerned, the less intrigue the better."

"Killjoy!" I tease, climbing into my car. "I'll e-mail you what I find *if* you promise to send me a return message confirming that you've received it. I'd hate to see all my sleuthing lost in the hundreds of messages you've let pile up in your inbox."

"Scout's honor." Lucy leans into the open car window and holds up three fingers in the Girl Scout pledge. "Liz, thanks again for being such a good friend. I've always been able to count on you."

"Me? You've got to be kidding, Lucy. Granted, I have great intentions, but I'm the one who's always losing her to-do list."

"Sweet Lizzie, when are you going to give yourself some credit?" she asks. Then she turns and walks up her driveway, leaving me in stunned silence.

■ ■ ■ ■

CHAPTER SEVEN

■ ■ ■ ■

Tom Ka Gai

3/4 pound boneless, skinless chicken breast
3 tablespoons vegetable oil
1 (14 oz.) can coconut milk
2 cups water
2 tablespoons fresh ginger, minced
4 tablespoons fish sauce
1/4 cup fresh lime juice
2 tablespoons chili sauce
1 small, hot red pepper
2 tablespoons green onion, thinly sliced
1 tablespoon chopped fresh cilantro

Instructions:

1. Cut chicken into thin strips and sauté in oil for 2–3 minutes.
2. In a pot, bring coconut milk and water to a boil. Reduce heat. Add ginger, fish sauce, lime juice, chili sauce and pepper. Simmer until

chicken is cooked through, 10–15 minutes.

3. Sprinkle with onion and fresh cilantro. Serve hot.

Pad Thai

1/2 lb. dried thin rice noodles
3 tablespoons fish sauce
3 or more tablespoons tamarind juice the thickness of fruit concentrate, to taste
2 tablespoons sugar
4 tablespoons vegetable oil
1/3 lb. fresh shrimp, shelled and deveined
4–5 cloves garlic, finely chopped
3 shallots, thinly sliced
1/4 cup sweetened salted radish, chopped
1–2 teaspoons ground dried red chilies
3 eggs
3 cups fresh bean sprouts
2/3 cup chopped, unsalted peanuts
1 lime, cut into small wedges
4 green onions, sliced

Instructions

1. Soak dried rice noodles in lukewarm water for 40 minutes to soften.
2. While the noodles are soaking, make sweet-and-sour seasoning by

mixing fish sauce with tamarind juice and sugar; stir well to melt the sugar. Set aside.

3. When the noodles have softened, drain and set aside. Heat a skillet or wok over high heat. Add 2 teaspoons oil and quickly stir-fry shrimp just until pink. Sprinkle lightly with fish sauce and remove from the pan.

4. Coat the skillet with remaining oil (except 1 teaspoon). Add garlic and sliced shallots. Cook for one minute. Add sweetened salted radish and ground dried chilies. Stir and heat through a few seconds.

5. Add noodles and toss well with the ingredients in the pan. Stir-fry 1–2 minutes. Push the mixture to one side of the pan. Add the remaining teaspoon of oil to the cleared area, crack the eggs onto it, and scramble lightly. Toss scrambled eggs with noodle mixture.

6. Add the reserved sweet-and-sour mixture. Stir well to evenly coat noodles. Taste and adjust flavors, if necessary, with more fish sauce, tamarind juice and/or sugar.

7. Toss noodles with 2 cups bean

sprouts. Add half the chopped peanuts and shrimp to the wok. Stir
until vegetables are partially wilted.
Transfer to a serving platter. Gar-
nish with remaining bean sprouts,
chopped peanuts, lime wedges and
green onions. Serves 4.

The next Tuesday, evidently prompted by Michael's bragging about his big night out with Jessie, John surprises me by planning a date night of our own. To break the news, he comes home from work an hour early, carrying a bouquet of flowers.

"So tell me," I say, placing the flowers in water while John rubs my shoulders, "what's the occasion?"

"Does there have to be an occasion to bring my lovely wife flowers?" he replies, nibbling on my ear. Little tingles run up my spine at the feel of his five o'clock shadow tickling the back of my neck.

"Um, no, but . . ." How do I gently say that my husband is not the kind of guy who would normally think to bring me flowers without the prompting of an officially sanctioned occasion?

"Well, since you asked," he persists, "I was hoping you would join me for dinner and a movie tonight."

"Tonight? Dinner *and* a movie? It's Tuesday!"

"Liz, there's no rule that says parents cannot go out together on a school night. I've already ordered a pizza for the kids and arranged for Katie to pick Hannah up from soccer."

"You're kidding!" I swivel to face him,

resting my wrists on his broad shoulders and loosely lacing my fingers behind his neck.

"No, I am not." His deep brown eyes sparkle with the pleasure of surprising me. "It's true, my dear. You are free of domestic encumbrance tonight. Now quick — get ready before something changes!"

I love it when John surprises me this way, but his thoughtfulness causes a predicament that would never occur to him, being a member of the male community. I have *nothing* to wear. Further complicating my anxiety, I can't utter a word about this conundrum. If I do, John might overhear and try to help.

I can hear him now: "You have plenty of clothes, Liz. What about these pants and this blouse? That looks great together. No, wait. Why don't you wear this? I love this dress."

Poor man. He hasn't a clue.

Unfortunately, in the midst of my wardrobe crisis, the last thing I have the time for is to explain to my husband the truth about a woman's wardrobe. In his naiveté, John assumes by my overstuffed closet that I have numerous outfits suitable for an evening out . . . when the reality of the situation is that I have *nothing* to wear.

John won't understand that the blue dress is too tight in the wrong places. Plus, he will never comprehend how finding out that I'm a "winter" completely excludes two-thirds of my wardrobe from consideration. (And yet I can't bear to give these items up because they are still "good" clothes. What would my laundry-loving mother think if I gave away a perfectly good sweater because my color consultant told me it was wrong for my skin tone? Mom probably never even heard of a color consultant.) Then there's the shoe issue. I can't wear my black slides with brown slacks — as if I could even consider the brown slacks, which obviously only work for "autumns." Yikes! It's hard being a woman!

Ten minutes later, with a pile of discarded clothing littering my bedroom, I finally decide on a pale blue sweater and black pants. The sweater is actually a "summer" color, but it is still in the "cool" family. I've been told that a "winter" wearing a "summer" color isn't a major fashion faux pas.

As I complete a series of deep-knee bends, designed to stretch out the seat of my pants, I wonder why deciding on an appropriate outfit is such a production. John seems to be happy regardless of what I wear. In fact, he rarely says anything unless I specifically ask for his opinion. I think his hesitancy stems from an exchange early in our marriage . . .

"How do I look, sweetheart?" I asked, doing a little twirl in a new dress I had bought for a friend's wedding.

"Fine," he replied in a distracted tone as he perused the day's mail.

"Fine?" I asked with a bit of hysteria creeping into my voice. "What's wrong? Does this dress make me look fat?"

"No, Liz, I said you look FINE."

"Not good or great? Just *fine?*" On the verge of panic, my heart was now hammering wildly in my chest.

John scratched his head. "Good. Great. Fine. What's the difference?"

"John, come on! Everyone knows what 'fine' *really* means!"

And with those words, I fled to the bedroom to change clothes, leaving John in serious doubt about his knowledge of vocabulary . . .

It took me a lot of years to realize that men just don't understand the fragility of a woman's ego when it comes to her appearance. I know I'll never stack up to a Hollywood hottie, but I am definitely passable for a woman over forty. And while a few of my body parts may be a bit worse for the wear, at least they're original. The bane of my existence, however, is my hair. And not just on certain days. Every day is a bad hair day at my bathroom mirror.

In spite of trying everything from setting my drab, brown hair with soup cans in junior high school to, most recently, over-heating my tresses with my daughter's flatiron, my hair is totally unruly. Who says those of us with naturally curly hair are the lucky ones? My dream is to wake up one morning with a head of lush locks falling to my waist in a silky sheet, like one of those hair-product commercials.

Every time I see actress Julianne Moore shaking her thick red hair and saying she's "worth it," I can't help but feel a flush of envy. No amount of crème conditioner will ever make *my* hair ripple. The best I can do is invest in a set of snazzy ponytail holders — and a variety of hats.

Peering into my mirror, I realize my skin still looks pretty good unless, as I recently found out, I happen to lose weight. While working on a column about new beauty products, one of my sources told me that overweight people appear to have smoother skin because fat deposits plump up wrinkles. As you can imagine, that little tidbit does nothing for my will power. Cheesecake or wrinkles? You decide.

Regardless of hair, weight, and/or future wrinkles, I can count on John to tell me that I have a "natural beauty" regardless of what I wear or slather on my face. Of course, I don't believe him, but it's always nice to hear.

Tonight we agree there will be no talk of kids, dogs, or bad hair allowed. We both feel the need to reconnect. In my opinion that means staring at each other in dim candle-light. In John's, it's sitting next to each other in the flickering light of the movie theater. Tonight we intend to do both.

"So where do you want to go for dinner?" he asks as we walk to the car.

"Anywhere but Drucillina's. Clarenzo wants to fatten me up."

"You're kidding?"

This comment stops me in my tracks. "So you think I'm fat enough already?"

He frowns. "That's not what I meant, Liz. It just surprised me that Clarenzo —"

"Better stop while you're ahead, don't you think, Johnny?" I interrupt, winking at him to lighten the mood.

"Definitely. You pick the restaurant. You always keep up on the good places to eat. No hidden meaning intended." He grins and opens the car door for me.

And we drive away, feeling like a couple of teenagers — albeit older, wiser teenagers — on a date again. We know the benefits of getting to bed by eleven o'clock.

John and I have dinner at Tasty Thailand — a great little restaurant located in the rear of an Asian market. As is our custom, we decide to share soup and an entrée instead of ordering separate meals. This makes it easier for me to justify dessert and usually brings a smile to John's face when he peruses the check at the end of the meal. John's not tight, but let's just say he likes to wring as much as possible out of a dollar.

We begin with a volcano pot of our favorite soup — Tom Ka Gai. John describes this soup as "a symphony in my mouth." I'm not exactly sure what he means, but it sounds so poetic that I always heartily agree. We choose spicy Pad Thai noodles topped with chopped peanuts for the main course and finish up with a bowl of sweet rice and juicy mango. Pleasantly full and somewhat sleepy, we opt to skip the movie and have a latte at a neighborhood coffee bar.

■ ■ ■ ■

At the counter I order my usual venti decaf hazelnut latte skinny. Marina told me this is the correct way to order when you'd like your drink made with skim, instead of whole, milk. I actually prefer whole milk, but I always feel chic saying "skinny." In my opinion, moms need to suck up every opportunity for chicness they come across.

"What can I make for you, sir?" asks the young barista, turning to my husband.

"Uhhh . . . just a cup of coffee," he replies.

"Café Americano?"

"Is that plain coffee?"

"Café Americano is made with espresso and hot water."

Noticing the blank look on John's face, she adds helpfully, "That's what most people who want regular coffee order."

"That'll be fine, then."

"What size would you like?"

"Uhhh . . . regular."

"We have grande or venti."

He chuckles. "I'll splurge. Give me a grande."

When we sit down at our small table, I notice John scowling at his coffee. "What's wrong?" I ask.

"Nothing."

Silence. More scowling. This time at my cup too.

"It's just that I hate what's happened to coffee," he finally admits.

"What? You don't like your coffee? You haven't even tasted it."

"That's not it. It's just that I ordered a grande . . . and your cup is larger."

"I ordered a venti. That's larger than grande."

"That's my point! How is a person supposed to know venti is larger than grande? Who has ever heard of a venti?"

"Well . . ."

"It's gotten so you have to know a foreign language just to order a cup of coffee. And I'd like to know what happened to free refills. Did you notice they charge fifty cents for a refill . . . regardless of cup size?" The naturally frugal side of my husband is indignant.

"Well . . . ," I begin to explain.

"This whole coffee thing has gotten ridiculous." He taps his index finger on the table. A sure sign he is starting to get really wound up. "It all started with McDonalds. Remember when they changed the drink size from 'small' to 'regular' on the menu?"

"I'm not —"

"Do they think people are idiots? Do they think we don't realize when they hand a regular cup out the window that we can't tell it's really a small?"

I take a sip of my venti latte. "Well . . ."

"And now the coffee shops list sizes in a foreign language," he says, shaking his head. "I'm just about ready to go back to gas-station coffee."

I give my exasperated husband a sympathetic smile, knowing after twenty years of marriage when it's best to leave a subject alone. The last thing I want to do is put a damper on our evening. After all, it's 9:15 on a Tuesday night, and we are still on a date. Just the *two* of us. Woo-hoo!

CHAPTER EIGHT

MARY ALICE'S CRANBERRY TUMBLE

2 eggs
1 1/2 cups granulated (white) sugar
1/2 teaspoon vanilla
1 cup flour
1/2 cup butter, melted
3 cups cranberries (fresh or frozen — but
  not dried)
1/2 cup chopped pecans (optional)

Instructions

1. Beat eggs until slightly thickened and lemony colored.
2. Add vanilla and 1 cup of the sugar. Mix in flour and melted butter.
3. Fold in rest of ingredients (cranberries and nuts, if desired), reserving 1/2 cup sugar.
4. Put batter in greased 8×8-inch pan. Sprinkle top of batter heavily with

163

remaining sugar.

5. Bake at 350 degrees for approximately 45 minutes or until golden brown and toothpick inserted in center comes out clean.
6. Cool and cut into bars.

Liz's Baked Potato Soup

2/3 cup butter
1 medium onion, diced
6 large potatoes, cubed
4 cups milk
2 cups heavy cream
1/4 teaspoon red pepper
Salt and pepper to taste
4 green onions, sliced
10–12 strips bacon, cooked, drained, and crumbled
1 1/4 cups shredded cheddar cheese

Instructions

1. In a large pot over low heat, melt butter.
2. Sauté onion in butter until translucent and slightly browned.
3. Add potatoes and milk. Cook on low heat until potatoes are very tender.
4. Stir in cream and seasonings. To

thicken, mash potatoes slightly.

5. Serve hot — topped with onions, bacon, and cheese. Serves six.

It's Friday! This week FAC is at Mary Alice's, which probably means Cranberry Tumble — a melt-in-your-mouth concoction whose recipe even Marina hasn't been able to pry from our usually amenable hostess. Mary Alice says she found the recipe in her late aunt's file — labeled "secret." And we all know that when it comes to keeping a secret, M.A. will take it to her grave.

As I open the door to Mary Alice's cozy colonial home, I am not disappointed. The smell of sugar and cranberries fills the air. Once again, I revel in my decision to heed Clarenzo's advice and take a break from my low-carb regime. I had announced this decision to my family last night by serving a pot of my famous baked potato soup . . .

"So, Mom, what's the deal?" Katie peered at her bowl of soup in shock. "Are these real potatoes, or are they made out of some obscure soy product?"

"They're real, all right," I said. "I have declared October 'Back to Carbohydrates Month.' We'll go back to a healthier diet in November."

John groaned. "Great. Just in time for Thanksgiving. Can't wait to see what's on the menu this year."

OK, OK. I guess I'll never live down last

166

year's attempt at a "Healthy Harris Holiday."

"And what about December?" asked Josh, a hint of panic in his voice. "You're not going to make us eat healthy at Christmas, are you? Mom, that's un-American!"

"Mommy, do sugar cookies have carbs?" asked Hannah, my angel, who likes all desserts as long as they have brightly colored sprinkles.

Once again I knew what my New Year's resolution would be — and thanked God for the genius who invented the elastic waistband . . .

I'm the last one to arrive at FAC since I had to take Josh to an orthodontist appointment after school. Much to my surprise, the group is already in the midst of an animated discussion about our visit to Tredway last weekend.

Since I stink at keeping secrets, I'm extremely relieved to find that Lucy has obviously told the group about our little field trip. Plus, over the past week, I've done some research on the property, so I'm itching to talk about what I found.

"I just love old houses," says Mary Alice, passing around a plate of Cranberry Tumble. "When did you say it was built, Lucy?"

I slip into my usual chair at the kitchen table.

"Actually, I wasn't sure until our resident journalist here" — Lucy gestures, smiling at me — "used her connections at the paper to dig up some history for me."

I wave away her thanks. "I just ran a search on the property. I think it helped that the house had a name as well as an address. Plugging 'Locust Hill' into the search engine brought up news clips as well as the usual public records."

"It was fascinating to read about my family's history here in Nebraska. I can't thank you enough, Liz."

"Yeah, yeah, yeah," says Marina. "We all know Liz is an ace reporter, but enough already. I want details!"

"You'll be proud of me, Kelly." Lucy pulls a folder from her bag. "I actually started a file on Locust Hill."

"Duly noted . . . and impressed," says Kelly.

"OK, girls," Jess breaks in. "I'm starting to agree with Marina. Enough yada, yada. What'd you find out?"

"Well, Liz was right when she said the house was probably more than a hundred years old," Lucy reports. "Locust Hill was built in the 1860s by Aunt Bette's great-grandfather, Joseph Simmons. He and his wife, the former Emily Clarke, moved west with a group of Congregationalist settlers to establish the town of Tredway."

"Their story is fascinating," I add. "Like a novel that's hard to put down."

"Details, Liz," says Marina. "Don't keep us in suspense."

"I found out that Joseph and Emily met at Oberlin College in Ohio where they were both students."

"Really?" asks Jessie, pouring another glass of tea. "I thought colleges were same-sex at the time."

"That's what's so interesting," I continue. "Most colleges only admitted men. Oberlin was the first college in the nation to offer coeducational classes. The couple married shortly after graduation, and Joseph began a medical practice. Meanwhile, Emily became very involved in the Young Ladies Literary Society."

"A book club?" asks Mary Alice.

"No, actually the Literary Society was very active in the abolition movement before and during the Civil War," I explain. "They produced pamphlets to educate people about the horrors of slavery and spoke quite frequently at antislavery rallies."

Kelly lifts an eyebrow. "*Really?* It's so cool

to hear about women who were politically active . . . even before they had the right to vote."

"I know what you mean. Just in reading about the activities of the group, I found connections to a 'Who's Who' of female abolitionists, including Harriet Beecher Stowe, Angelina Grimke, and Mary Sheldon."

"I've heard those names," says Jessie. "I had the kids read *Uncle Tom's Cabin* by Harriet Beecher Stowe last spring, and it prompted Sarah to choose to do a project on the Underground Railroad. I remember reading about Grimke and Sheldon in her report. They were pretty gutsy ladies, especially for that time."

"Looks like you come from pretty strong stock, Luce," Marina announces. "Now I know where you get that stubborn streak." She gives Lucy a light punch on the shoulder.

Lucy laughs with more life in her voice than I've heard in months. "Behind every book club is a revolutionary."

"Actually, the Oberlin women were thought by some people to be quite revolutionary," I say, "but their values were very conservative. And rooted in a deep faith. In fact, the women eventually established what was called the Maternal Association for mothers to 'discuss and improve their practices for rearing godly and moral children.' "

"Sounds like MOPS without the crafts," Mary Alice comments.

"In a way. Older women of the community, particularly the wives of college faculty, served as mentors to the young moms. And from what I read, the men were so impressed that they formed their own auxiliary organization to mentor young men."

"Liz, where did you find all this out?" asks Lucy. "It wasn't in the material you sent me, was it? Or did I just miss it?"

"No," I admit a bit sheepishly. "I did some more research yesterday. Once I get going on a subject that piques my interest, it's hard for me to stop. Maybe I can work it into a column so I'll have an excuse for all the laundry I've been neglecting."

"Before we start commiserating about laundry," says Kelly, "I want to know what prompted your ancestors to move to Nebraska, Lucy."

"From what I've been able to figure out from the records, Joseph left a successful medical practice to bring Oberlin's philosophy west. He wanted to establish a Christian college."

Kelly furrows her brow. "I don't mean to be rude, but isn't it a little odd to start a college in the middle of nowhere?"

"It does seem a little ambitious, but they apparently got the school going. Tredway College was founded in 1861. Joseph Simmons is listed as one of the charter faculty members."

Jess whistles softly. "That's very impressive."

"Yeah, yeah, yeah . . . now let's get to the good stuff," Marina insists.

"Such as?" Lucy asks.

"Liz said Old Joe's story reads like a novel. All stories have juicy parts. You know, deception, intrigue, murder, mayhem . . . the good stuff."

"It seems my family is a bit lean on the murder and mayhem front, but they did experience some heartbreak. It looks like Emily and Joseph may have had some difficulty having children."

"I could only locate birth records for one child — Anna Louise," I say.

Lucy nods. "That's right. And it was very rare in those days for a family to have only one child."

"But that makes sense," Jess reasons. "It took a lot of work by everyone in the family just to survive during the pioneer era."

"Anna inherited Locust Hill after her parents died," says Lucy. "She married a circuit preacher named Jonathon Crawford in 1876. There are birth records for four stillborn children before my grandfather and Aunt Bette were born."

A pained expression crosses Mary Alice's face. "Four children were born dead? The poor woman."

"I suspect that may be part of the reason for Locust Hill's reputation," I add.

Marina sits forward. "What kind of reputation?"

I look at Lucy for permission to reveal my findings.

She rolls her eyes. "It's just a silly legend, but go ahead and tell them."

"It seems Locust Hill is thought to be a haunted house."

"Ooooo . . . ," says Marina.

Kelly shakes her head. "Give me a break."

"Liz, are you saying that people think the house is being haunted by Anna's babies?" asks Jess.

"I'm not really sure. I just came across an old newspaper clipping about Halloween traditions that referred to the property as Tredway's 'House on Haunted Hill.' "

"Well, I certainly didn't notice any ghostly

forms or floating orbs when we were at Locust Hill," Kelly chimes in.

I frown. "I didn't say the house is haunted . . . just that it has a spooky reputation. Maybe it's the reporter in me, but I'd like to know what's behind the mystery."

"Me too," agrees Marina. "So, Lucy, when are you going to introduce us to your mystery manor?"

"Well, it's hardly a manor, but it does have a certain amount of charm. And some good memories."

"Have you given any thought to what you'll do with the property?" Jess asks.

"Yes, quite a bit. In the last few days, actually. I'm not sure I'll end up keeping it, but I don't feel comfortable putting Locust Hill on the market right now. Besides, it needs some updating."

Mary Alice perks up. "Are you talking major restoration, Lucy, or just some freshening?"

Lucy looks at Kelly and me. "A little of both, don't you think?"

"The floors and woodwork are beautiful," Kelly says.

"And the house is full of some gorgeous old furniture," I add. "Lucy will have to beat the antique dealers off with a stick."

"It sounds wonderful," Mary Alice gushes.

"It is, but there's still a lot of work that needs to be done," says Kelly. "I recognized the dining-room wallpaper from one of my mother's childhood photos. I'd describe it as more shabby than chic."

"The kitchen is huge, but it doesn't have a dishwasher," I add. "Also there's only one bathroom. On the second floor."

"Aunt Bette must be pretty spry to live there as long as she did," Marina reflects. "I'm too spoiled to live with just one bathroom."

"It sounds like you'll need a contractor to update the kitchen and see about putting in a second bathroom," suggests Jessie. "But if the 'bones' are good, we could probably handle the rest."

"What do you mean by 'we,' Jess?" asks Lucy.

"You know what she means, Luce, and she's right," Kelly declares. "If we work together, we can get a lot done."

"I agree," says Marina. "Besides, ever since I watched *Trading Spaces* on television, I've had an itch to redo something."

"I wouldn't even know where to start," Lucy begins.

"I can ask around at the station about contractors," says Marina. "Cops are always looking for ways to moonlight. Gives 'em an excuse to flex their muscles."

"Great idea." Kelly pulls the ever-present day planner from her purse. "And Mary Alice has a flair for design. She can help pick out the paint and wallpaper."

"Kelly, I don't know if Lucy would like — ," Mary Alice protests.

"Quit being modest," orders Marina. "Just look at this place." She gestures flamboyantly around the tasteful, color-coordinated, well-organized room. "It's like something out of a magazine."

"You do have wonderful taste, Mary Alice," agrees Lucy, "but I wouldn't want to impose."

"Actually, Lucy, it would be a treat to help you. I love to decorate, but I'm afraid Craig will hit the roof if he finds the furniture rearranged again or new wallpaper in the bathroom."

"If you're sure it wouldn't be imposing on our friendship," says Lucy, "I'd love to have your help."

"I don't know what shape the grounds are in, but I could spruce up the landscaping," Jessie offers. "Besides, I love to dig in the dirt this time of year. Maybe I could put in a few bulbs for next spring?"

Lucy beams. "Jess, that sounds delightful."

"That settles it," says Kelly. "We've got our crew. All we need to do is set a date."

After some coaxing, Lucy agrees to schedule a working weekend at Locust Hill in place of our FAC fall retreat. Marina dubs it "Extreme Home Makeover: Locust Hill."

In the past, we've booked a hotel in a nearby city for our annual girls-only getaway. We call it a "shop and hop" since the weekend usually involves some serious shopping — and a good deal of restaurant hopping. This year, we agree to forgo the shopping to spend our days giving Locust Hill a face-lift. But when it comes to food, we decide not to break tradition.

"Liz, you can be in charge of food," Kelly announces, writing my name down on her planning sheet.

"Great idea!" Marina booms.

"Wait a minute," I say. "Don't we usually go out for meals?"

"Yes." Kelly's voice is dripping with patience. "But there is usually more than one restaurant in town."

"But you must have forgotten, Kelly," I reply, shooting her my best impression of the proverbial evil eye. "The kitchen at Locust Hill is a bit dated. It doesn't even have a dishwasher."

"Then we'll use paper plates." She returns

my look with an even more withering one and snaps her planner shut. Subject closed.

I open my mouth to protest, but the words freeze in my throat. I know when I'm beat. Arguing with Kelly is like trying to fill a bucket that's full of holes. I might as well accept that I'll be cooking for an entire weekend in a kitchen built before the Civil War — with appliances from the Roaring Twenties. What I wouldn't give to strip wallpaper instead . . .

■ ■ ■ ■

CHAPTER NINE

■ ■ ■ ■

Johnny's Quick 'n' Easy Lasagna

1 lb. ground beef and/or Italian sausage
6 cups meatless spaghetti sauce
8 oz. lasagna noodles, uncooked
16 oz. ricotta cheese
12 oz. mozzarella cheese, shredded
1/2 cup grated Parmesan cheese

Instructions

1. In large pan, brown ground beef and/or sausage. Add spaghetti sauce. Simmer 15 minutes.
2. In a 13×9×2-inch pan, spread 1 cup of sauce. Then alternate layers of lasagna noodles (uncooked), ricotta, sauce, mozzarella, and Parmesan cheese. End with sauce, mozzarella, and Parmesan. Cover with foil.
3. Bake at 350 degrees for 50 minutes until lightly browned and bubbling.

Remove foil and cook for 10 more minutes until noodles are softened, but firm.

4. Let stand 15 minutes. Cut in squares to serve. Makes 8 servings.

I am officially a nervous wreck. Josh needs "something good" to contribute to the youth group bake sale at church tomorrow morning, FAC is counting on me to come up with a creative menu for the weekend in Tredway, and my turn to host Dinner Club is coming up.

I rue the day we decided to forgo making this monthly gathering of college friends a potluck affair and instead assigning the host couple sole responsibility for planning and preparing a dinner for sixteen. Our reasoning, that this system only required each couple to cook once every eight months, seemed logical when we were newlyweds. But with three kids and a dog complicating my life, pulling off my turn at Dinner Club is always a feat. And, to make matters worse, my column is due on Monday morning.

The problem is that I don't know what to do first. I need to go to the grocery store to buy ingredients for Josh's bake-sale contribution, but I still have to decide what to make. I also need to send out invitations to Dinner Club, but I've procrastinated, and now I'm wondering if I should just call everyone instead. I also have no idea what to cook for the party — much less when I'll have time to clean the house. With all this rattling around in my head, I don't have time to even think about our FAC weekend, but I keep obsessing about it anyway.

What is wrong with me? Organized Kelly and creative Mary Alice would already have lists and timetables drawn up. Jess can usually figure out a way to work much of the preparation for a party into learning projects for her kids. Lucy, a natural hostess, seems to entertain effortlessly. And Marina has such a strong personality that no one cares about cobwebs or table decorations. Me? I'm immobilized — and growing more anxious by the minute.

Enter my well-meaning husband, John, who always tries valiantly to solve my problems. He suggests we pick up a pie from the grocery store for Josh's bake sale and even offers to make a pan of his Quick 'n' Easy Lasagna for Dinner Club. It's tempting, but I can't bring myself to take his way out. Why? I hate admitting this, but it all stems from the abhorrent *P* word — *PRIDE.*

Ever since I started writing my newspaper column, "The Lovely Life," I've felt the need to appear as this *amazing* cook and *clever* hostess. The only problem is that I'm just an average cook — and not overly clever — so I've done everything I can to keep these facts from public view.

Today, standing over my kitchen sink, it dawns on me. I've become paralyzed by the expectation of perfection. *That's it,* I decide. *Enough is enough.*

I whiz into the study, flip on my computer, and wait on the edge of my seat for it to boot up. And then I begin typing furiously.

```
The Lovely Life
By Elizabeth Harris
Dear Readers,
   This may be the last time you
read my column. What is the
reason for this rather star-
tling and unexpected state-
ment? Today I must make what
may be, for many fans of "The
Lovely Life," a very disquiet-
ing confession. I can no
longer live with the cha-
rade  .  .  .  the great
farce . . . the sham . . . that
has become my public image.
   Please believe me, I didn't
intend for this to happen. I'm
not even sure when the situa-
tion began to snowball. The
simple fact is this: I can no
longer hold up — either physi-
cally or emotionally — under
```

the pressure of my public persona. I have to "come clean," as they say in criminal circles, fully realizing that I may lose many of the faithful readers I hold close to my heart.

So, without further delay, I post my confession boldly — for all the world to see.

MY NAME IS NOT "MARTHA."

IN FACT, I AM ABOUT AS FAR FROM BEING A DOMESTIC DIVA AS ONE CAN GET.

There! I've said it! The proverbial cat is out of the bag! And, I must admit, it feels fabulous! I suspect some of my faithful readers may not share this joy — and perhaps harbor a hope this is a great exaggeration. For those readers, I feel compelled to present the following "Top Ten List" as proof of my domestic ineptitude:

1. I have never made a radish "rose" or dressed a strawberry in a chocolate "tux-

edo."

2. I am hopeless when it comes to craft projects. In fact, I have an acute fear of glue guns after an unfortunate incident involving dried flowers and raffia.

3. I have not alphabetized my spices.

4. There are plastic containers in my cupboards without lids — and lids without containers.

5. Each fall I plan to plant spring bulbs in my garden but have yet to actually do it. More than one box of bulbs, intended for planting, has rotted in my garage.

6. I have never had my air ducts professionally cleaned. (Please do not e-mail me about what is likely living in the ductwork. As the mother of two teenagers, I have enough to keep me awake at night.)

7. I once created a toxic cloud in my home by mixing

up a cleaning solution of ammonia and chlorine bleach, prompting a trip to the emergency room.

8. I despise doing laundry and sometimes surreptitiously raid my husband's underwear drawer in a desperate search for clean lingerie. (Can a pair of men's briefs even be considered lingerie?)

9. I do not tie my sheet sets with a satin ribbon or stack them neatly in the linen closet. In fact, our "linen closet" is stuffed with shoeboxes and grocery sacks containing photos from the last twenty years.

10. The idea of scrapbooking instills me with such panic that my throat begins to tighten. (What if I die in an accident and Hannah discovers I haven't finished her baby book?)

Yes, it's true. A Domestic Diva I will never be. However,

I am convinced that shedding this image provides a wonderful opportunity for the future of this column.

Join me in throwing off pretense. Celebrate being REAL women — without perfect cupboards and pedicures! Women who would love to serve their families ossobuco with roasted seasonal vegetables, but realistically reach for the Hamburger Helper! Women who love their families, but sometimes need their own space!

Faithful readers, I give you this solemn promise. My next column (if I still have one) will contain practical ideas and advice to help make the most of the time and abilities with which we are all uniquely blessed. REAL WOMEN UNITE!

As I clicked Send, shooting my column through cyberspace to my editor, I wondered if the paper would even run this piece. Perhaps the editorial board would decide to quietly retire the column — and its obviously loony author.

But I didn't care. I was savoring the sweet taste of freedom. Snatching my car keys from the counter, I headed toward the garage. After all, I had to talk to a man about a pan of lasagna — and pick up a pie at the grocery store.

■ ■ ■ ■

CHAPTER TEN

■ ■ ■ ■

PANINI

3/4 cup Italian salad dressing
8 oz. prosciutto, thinly sliced
8 oz. roasted turkey or chicken, thinly sliced
12 slices mozzarella cheese
12 tomato slices
12 large fresh basil leaves
12 slices Italian bread

Instructions

1. Layer prosciutto, turkey or chicken, mozzarella, tomato slices, and basil on six slices of bread.
2. Drizzle lightly with dressing.
3. Press top slice of bread on top. Brush both top and bottom of bread with dressing.
4. Grill panini on both sides until lightly browned and cheese is melted.

5. Cut sandwiches in half to serve.

Liz's Cold Broccoli Salad

3/4 cup salad dressing or mayonnaise
2 tablespoons sugar
2 tablespoons vinegar
1 medium bunch broccoli, separated into bite-sized florets
6–8 slices cooked bacon, crumbled
1/2 cup red onion, chopped
1/2 cup raisins (optional)

Instructions

1. Mix salad dressing or mayonnaise, sugar, and vinegar in large bowl.
2. Add remaining ingredients; mix lightly.
3. Refrigerate 1 hour or until ready to serve.

Our FAC weekend has finally arrived. And none too soon for me. I'm in bliss just thinking about a whole three days with girlfriends . . . and no teenagers. I lean my head back — face soaking up the late October sun — as we cruise along the country roads in Marina's blue convertible. There's nothing better than fall in the Midwest. Granted, we have our share of nasty blizzards and hot summer days here in Nebraska, but the languorous change of seasons makes it all worthwhile.

"So what time did Mary Alice and Lucy leave this morning?" asks Jessie, who is sitting next to me in the backseat.

"About ten, I think." I open one eye and see that Jess looks as relaxed as I feel. Clothed in her husband's oversized denim shirt — chestnut curls billowing and the autumn sun glancing off her face — she is the picture of serenity.

Jessie is just a few years older than I am (although I'd never say so for fear of offending her). She is who I hope to be when I "grow up." Really. Jess is one of those people who's comfortable in her own skin. She has strong convictions and isn't afraid to tell you how she feels. But she does it in a gentle way that has you leaning forward in your chair to hear more. I reach across the seat and squeeze Jessie's hand — a silent acknowledgment of how much I treasure her and our friendship.

The four of us — Marina, Kelly, Jess, and I — are on the way to Tredway and Locust Hill. The two other members of our group had loaded up Mary Alice's SUV with paint, wallpaper, and tools and were already there.

At our last FAC, Kelly said we needed to hit the ground running at Locust Hill to be most effective — and attempting to get six women to leave on time for a weekend trip would be a logistical nightmare. Thus, Lucy and Mary Alice, who have the most flexible schedules, volunteered to serve as the advance team for our project.

"I hope they didn't forget anything this morning," says Kelly from the front passenger seat.

"How could they, Kel?" I tease. "You put the supply list on a spreadsheet and e-mailed it to Home Depot. I think you have the bases covered, sweetie."

"Turn here, Marina," Kelly orders, ignoring my teasing. "The house is just up this road at the top of the hill."

"I see it now," Marina says after turning onto Locust Ave. "It looks a little lonely up there, doesn't it?"

Kelly smirks. "What were you expecting? To find a haunted house in the 'burbs?"

It takes us awhile to untangle ourselves and all the paraphernalia we've brought for the weekend. But finally we all start up the driveway toward the house.

Jessie pauses for a moment on the gravel drive and gazes up toward the sky. "Look at all these beautiful old trees."

"I suspect most were planted by Anna's husband," I say. "According to the newspaper clips I read, he became quite an arborist — probably influenced by J. Sterling Morton, who lived not far from here in Nebraska City."

Jess nods. "You're probably right. Morton started Arbor Day around that time."

"Morton's the salt guy, isn't he? The box with the little girl and the umbrella?" asks Marina. "What do you think made a guy in the salt business turn into such a tree hugger?"

"I'm guessing you didn't grow up around here."

I jump at the sound of the deep voice behind us. We all turn to see the source of the comment.

The man who's walking up the hill behind us is tall. He looks to be in his midforties and has the easy stride and wiry body of someone who works with his hands. As he comes closer, I'm startled by his bright blue eyes — a stark contrast to a deeply tanned face that looks like it's been cured by the sun.

"Who are you?" Marina demands, putting a hand to her belt and affecting what I've come to refer to as her tough-cop persona.

"Sure you want to know?" answers the stranger, a hint of amusement in his eyes. "I might be one of those tree huggers you were talking about."

"Are you?" asks Marina.

"Maybe." He doesn't break her stare. "As I said, if you were from around here, you'd be a little more grateful for old man Morton. Without him and Arbor Day, this area might still be a treeless plain instead of the lush landscape you ladies were just complimenting."

"It's getting so a person can't even make a joke without the PC police swooping down," grumbles Marina, looking away and shaking her head.

"I know you didn't mean any harm, but this subject's a little sensitive for me. My family has farmed west of here for three generations. If it weren't for the trees, the wind would have taken the land a long time ago."

"Hey, I'm sorry," says Marina in a more congenial tone. "I'm just a city girl with a big mouth. Why don't we start over?"

"No problem." He chuckles.

"Well . . . who are you?"

"Jeff Taylor's the name. I'm the contractor you hired last week. That is, if you are the infamous Lieutenant Favazza."

Marina's jaw drops.

He grins. "Your big-city accent gave you away."

For one of the first times I can remember, Marina appears speechless.

Jessie breaks the uncomfortable silence. "Well, Mr. Taylor, I can see that you come by your affection for wood naturally."

"I guess you could say that. So, Lieutenant" — Jeff turns to face Marina — "have I lost the job?"

A bit flustered, but apparently unwilling to admit she may have met her match, Marina assured Jeff that she was perfectly willing to give him a fair shake, regardless of his political leanings. Right now she and Lucy are showing him around the house while Kelly supervises the rest of us in unloading the supplies.

Kelly's in her element and on a roll. "Let's use the kitchen as a staging area. Just put everything in there as you unload. I'll check it off my list as it comes off the truck."

"Wait a minute, Kel," I break in. "If we store the supplies in the kitchen, where am I supposed to cook?"

"Liz, you know I love you, but this cooking issue is beginning to grate on me."

"But —"

"You'll figure something out."

I bite my tongue, remembering my commitment not to "sweat the small stuff." Tonight I won't even bother cooking. We'll have sandwiches. No big deal.

I am calm.

I am relaxed.

I *will* be serene.

Even if it kills me.

As I'm making my sixth trek down the narrow front corridor of the house with a paint can in each hand and a plastic sack of brushes pinned under my arm, I hear a loud *CRACK!*

"What in the world," I mutter, racing toward where the sound appears to have originated. As I turn the corner into the kitchen, I see Jeff has wedged a crowbar between the wall and a built-in cupboard.

200

He and Marina are using the tool as a lever in an attempt to pry the cupboard away from the wall. Meanwhile, Lucy is on the floor, frantically running her hands along the woodwork at the base of the cabinet.

I pause in the doorway. "I thought demolition didn't start till tomorrow."

"Liz, get over here," grunts Marina. "We need your help."

"What are you trying to do?"

"I'll explain in a minute." Marina's voice is strained, and so are her muscles. "Just drop the stuff and get over here. Quick! I don't want to lose our leverage."

"Liz, we need you to feel around the bottom lip of the soffit above us," Jeff explains. "We're looking for some sort of latch . . . or maybe a button."

"OK." I set the paint and brushes down and pull one of the tall kitchen stools toward the cabinet. "What do you want me to do if I find something?"

"Unlatch it," says Marina. "And could you do it before I throw my back out?"

I climb up on the stool and run my hands along the painted wood. Lucy does the same thing below. We comb every inch of the cupboard and woodwork without success.

"I don't think we're going to find anything," I report after several minutes.

"We're going to have to force it then," says Jeff. "Got anything left, Marina? Think we can pop this baby?"

"I don't know, but let's give it a shot."

"OK. On three. One. Two. Ready? *Three.*"

The groans of Jeff and Marina mingle with the sound of splitting wood as they attempt to pry the cabinet from the wall. All of a sudden, there's a sharp *thwap,* like a thick spring has snapped.

"There it is," says Jeff. "I knew there had to be a latch. Someone had boxed over it. We should be able to move the cabinet now."

As we stare with wide eyes, Jeff slowly swings open the cupboard like a door. A cloud of dust filters into the room, causing him to cough. Pulling a flashlight from his tool belt, Jeff peers into the darkness behind the wall.

"Well, I'll be . . ." He whistles.

"What?" Marina demands, walking closer to peer over his shoulder.

"It looks like a little room."

"A storage room?" asks Lucy. "Maybe something from an earlier renovation?"

"Well, there's only one way to find out." Marina unceremoniously tries to elbow her way into the room.

Jeff holds out his arm, effectively barring her from the space. "Why don't you let me check it out first?"

"Listen, Bubba," Marina sputters, "I've got a gun strapped to my ankle. I think I can handle it."

"Marina!" I hiss.

"No, she's right." Jeff steps aside. "It's better to let a trained professional investigate. You're not afraid of possums, are you, Marina? Or river rats? You never know what you'll find in the walls of an old house."

Marina looks over her shoulder and — of all things — sticks out her tongue.

"So much for our trained professional," I mutter as she heads into the chamber.

"Liz, I'm going to scream if I hear you say, 'What in the world?' one more time," Marina complains. "You're a journalist, for heaven's sake! How 'bout a little variety?"

"Just for that comment, my friend, there will be no panini for you tonight!" I set a platter of the hot sandwiches down with a *thump* on the long kitchen table that already holds my colorful Cold Broccoli Salad.

"Panini? Now the girl thinks she's Italian!" teases Marina.

I'm grateful for Marina's attempt to lighten the mood. We are all a little edgy after sorting through the strange collection of articles she and Jeff discovered in the space behind the cupboard.

From what they could see in the dim light, the tiny room is about 4×6 feet in size. Stacked in a far corner was a chest filled with old clothes and blankets, a stoneware water jug, and some sort of rusty apparatus. Stuffed behind the chest, was a tattered quilt with a large dark stain.

Mary Alice gingerly fingered the quilt. "What do you think motivated someone to save this?"

"Whoever kept this old rag certainly didn't read your column on getting rid of clutter, Liz," says Kelly, peering at the faded fabric.

Jess pokes Kelly in the side with her elbow. "Hey! Remember, Kel, one person's trash is another's treasure."

"I really feel sorry for the family that considered this old quilt a treasure. It's not only a pile of rags — it has brown stains all over it."

"Let me see, M.A.," says Jess, motioning to Mary Alice to pass the quilt across the table. "It almost looks like . . ." A small gasp escapes from her lips.

"Jess?" asks Kelly. "What . . ." I see Jess cut her off with a quick flick of her hand.

This piques my interest and brings me right back to my days as a cub reporter covering the police beat. *Could the brown stains possibly be blood? Is that what caused Jess to shut Kelly up?*

Before I can investigate, Lucy has a question of her own. "What could this have been used for?" she asks, holding up a thick piece of rusty chain that is riveted to a crudely made iron band.

"Jeff, you're the carpenter," says Kelly. "Is it some sort of tool?"

"It's like no tool I've ever used. I hate to say this, but I think Marina may have had more experience with this kind of thing."

We all look at Marina who, it suddenly occurs to me, has been uncharacteristically quiet ever since we began to sift through the dusty contents of the hidden room.

"So, Rina," Kelly asks, "what is this?"

"I'm not positive, but it could be . . ." Marina stops speaking and looks down at her hands.

"What, Marina?" Lucy prompts. "Tell me what you think this is."

"Lucy, I have an idea, but I might be wrong. I really should do a little research before I go spouting off like —"

Lucy cuts her off sharply. "Marina, please. Since when have you ever been afraid to speak up? I need to know what you think."

"Luce, as I said, I could be way off here.

But if I had to guess, I'd say this was once part of a set of handcuffs . . . or shackles, as they used to be called."

"Shackles?" I ask. "What would shackles be doing —"

Marina cuts me off with a stern look as I begin to put the pieces together. Clothing. Blankets. A water jug. Shackles. Is it possible that someone once used this room as a secret prison cell? As I study the faces around the table, I suspect the same thought is occurring to each of my friends.

Lucy breaks the silence. "Well, girls, I hate to put a damper on our weekend, but I have no desire to spend the night in a house of horrors."

"Now, Lucy," says Jess, taking one of Lucy's thin hands in both of her own, "there are a lot of possible explanations for what we've found."

"It's the curse of reality TV," Marina mutters. "Everybody thinks she's an investigator. Jess is right, Lucy. There are a million scenarios that could explain what we found in that room."

"Such as?" Tears brim on Lucy's lashes.

Seeing Lucy's tears just about breaks my heart. This was supposed to be a fun weekend. A way to get Lucy out of the house — and her mind off her problems. Some dark family secret is the last thing she needs. *This just isn't fair. Come on, God. How about giving her a break?*

"See?" Marina adds. "That's a perfect example of what I'm trying to say. The problem with amateur detectives is that they start laying out possible scenarios before they have all the facts. The first rule of investigation is to let the facts tell you the story. And right now we have very few of those."

"You go, girl," I tease. "Now you do sound like a professional."

Marina shoots me a sarcastic look across the table. "The first thing we need to do is talk to the people who might have some knowledge about the room. Now, who would be on the short list?"

"There's Aunt Bette," says Jess. "She lived here most of her life."

"And Janelle," I add. "I also might be able to find something at the Cramer County Historical Society. Maybe some architectural drawings for the original structure. They have an office at the library downtown."

"See? We've already got some good leads," Marina insists. "Why don't we dig into this great food Liz has made and then talk about where to begin in the morning?"

Lucy puts her head in her hands. "I don't think I can stay in this house overnight." Her words are muffled. "I wouldn't be able to sleep wondering if someone who was related to me could have —"

"Stop it right now, Lucy," Kelly demands, slapping her hand down on the table. "As Marina says, we need to gather the facts. Instead of sitting around, I say we go see Aunt Bette right now."

"Kelly, I can't — ," Lucy tries.

Kelly's frown deepens. "Yes, you can. Come on, Liz, we'll take Mary Alice's SUV. You don't mind, do you, M.A.?"

"Whatever you —"

"Great. The rest of you can get started here. I've already laid out a work plan. It's posted on the refrigerator. Any questions?"

We all sit in stunned silence — me with my mouth open — staring at our friend in full commandant mode.

"Good. Grab a sandwich and let's go," Kelly says, pulling Lucy gently but firmly from her chair. She shoots me "the look" as they head toward the door. "Come on, Liz. We don't have all day."

■ ■ ■ ■

CHAPTER ELEVEN

■ ■ ■ ■

How to Brew a Perfect Pot of Tea

1. Bring fresh, cold water to a rolling boil.
2. Preheat teapot by pouring a little boiling water into it and allow it to sit for a few seconds. Discard water.
3. Place one tea bag or one teaspoon of loose tea per cup of water in teapot.
4. Pour hot water over tea and allow to steep for the correct amount of time.

Steeping Time

Green Tea: 3 minutes
Black Tea: 5 minutes
Herbal Tea: 6 minutes

Simple Shortbread

1 cup butter, room temperature
1/2 cup powdered sugar
2 cups sifted flour

Instructions:

1. Cream butter with sugar.
2. Add flour until well combined.
3. Press into greased 10-inch pie or tart pan. Mark into 12 wedges. Sprinkle with mixture of 1/4 teaspoon cinnamon and 1/4 cup sugar, if desired.
4. Bake at 300 degrees for 30 minutes. Cut while warm.

"I always suspected there was a secret room," says Aunt Bette.

Lucy's aunt seems to be in another world as we sit on the veranda of her new home at the Pacific Meadows Retirement Community. The setting sun is lighting the sky with thick bands of color ranging from pale pink to deep purple. Although the surroundings are serene, Lucy, Kelly, and I are far from calm.

Kelly's lead foot brought us to the tiny town of Orrick in record time. We had found Aunt Bette in the garden, finishing an after-dinner stroll with another resident. She was hard to miss with a brightly patterned shawl wrapped around her tiny frame — a colorful barrier to the chill of the autumn evening. As she approached, the setting sun backlit her wispy white hair, making it look like the halos common in religious art. She greeted Lucy with open arms and seemed not at all surprised by our visit. Or Lucy's description of the gruesome discovery behind the kitchen wall.

"What would make you think there might have been a secret room at Locust Hill, Aunt Bette?" Lucy asks, jarring the old woman from her private musings. "Now I'm more confused than ever."

"Of course you are, dear. I'm so sorry.

Let me start from the beginning."

"Frankly, after finding all those ghastly things behind the wall, I'm not sure I want to hear the entire story."

"Of course you do, Lucy," says Kelly. "That's why we're here." Apparently noticing Lucy isn't quite convinced, Kelly asks pointedly, "Right, Liz?"

"Umm, I guess." How easily I slip into my role as agreeable sidekick.

"I'm beginning to think it was a mistake coming here," Lucy says with a tremor in her voice. "Or even coming to Tredway at all."

"No, no, dear, you did the right thing. You needed to come — especially now."

"Why now?" Lucy massages her temples as if her head aches. "I'm not sure I can take much more."

"Lucy, I may be an old woman with old-fashioned ideas, but some things hold true through the generations. And this is one of them. Although it's not always easy, my dear, we need to understand where we came from if we want to move forward."

"How will it help to find out I come from a line of sadistic monsters?" Lucy moans.

"Come on, Lucy," Kelly scolds. "You don't know that."

Lucy takes a long breath and presses the

heels of her hands to her eyes. "Honestly, I just don't know if I'm up to this."

"I understand how upset and confused you must be right now," says the old woman gently. "I only ask that you try to keep an open mind. Things are not always as they appear at first glance."

"You sound like Marina," mumbles Lucy.

"Marina?"

"She's one of our friends . . . a police officer," I explain. "Marina's the one who helped uncover the room and its contents this afternoon. She said not to make any assumptions until we have all the facts."

Aunt Bette's eyes twinkle. "Well, she sounds like a wise young woman. You should listen to her advice."

"Miss Crawford, please don't repeat that in front of Marina," says Kelly. "Her ego will swell more than one of her mama's ravioli."

Aunt Bette laughs. It's a warm, musical sound that fills the veranda, prompting other residents to smile. "I promise. But only if you will also do a favor for me."

"What's that?"

"Call me Aunt Bette. Miss Crawford is much too formal."

"No problem. Aunt Bette it is," Kelly promises.

"Thank you, dear. Now where were we?"

"You were just about to reveal the diseased roots of our family tree," Lucy murmurs sarcastically, looking away.

"Lucy, come on," Kelly chides. "This cynicism isn't at all like you."

"Perhaps you don't know the real me, Kelly. I obviously have a few skeletons in the closet."

"Dear child," says Aunt Bette, "suspecting the worst is not going to help at all. Just indulge me and listen with an open mind. I think you'll be surprised with what you find."

Lucy's head whips around. "I've had enough surprises, don't you think?" Her eyes now sparkle with anger, instead of tears.

"Yes, of course you have," Aunt Bette soothes. "That was a poor choice of words, my dear. I'd just like the opportunity to pass along a little family history. Then I have something to give you that will help to answer your questions. After that, you are free to make up your own mind. Is that fair?"

"Yes, of course, Aunt Bette. I don't mean to be rude, it's just that . . ."

The deep wrinkles in Aunt Bette's face crinkle as her lips form a gentle smile. "No need for explanations, my dear. But down deep you want to know the truth, don't you?"

"I guess."

"One of my favorite memory verses from Sunday school is from the Gospel of John. It reads, 'You will know the truth, and the truth will make you free.' "

"Of course, you're right. And even if you weren't, my bullheaded friends wouldn't let me rest until I hear the whole story. So let's just get on with it."

"I believe you are making the right decision, dear. But first, why don't I ask Emma to bring us a nice pot of tea?"

When the sun sets, the outside temperature begins to drop. Aunt Bette suggests we move inside to a cozy corner of the spacious sitting room at Pacific Meadows.

As we settle into our chairs, a young girl approaches, carrying a tray laden with a tea service and a beautifully arranged plate of shortbread.

"This looks lovely, Emma, thank you. By the way, I don't think you've met my great-niece, Lucy. And these are her friends, Liz and Kelly. They are staying at Locust Hill this weekend."

The young woman bows her head shyly.

"Nice to meet you." Then she addresses Lucy. "I recognize you from the photo in Miss Crawford's room."

"You keep a photo of me in your room?" says Lucy, turning to Aunt Bette.

"Of course, dear. My memory isn't as good as it used to be. It helps me remember to pray for you."

"Janelle mentioned that when we visited Locust Hill the first time. She said you put me on the prayer chain at church."

"I learned a long time ago that the best thing you can do for those you love is to pray for them."

"That means a lot to me, Aunt Bette. Thank you."

The old woman pats Lucy's hand with her own wrinkled one. "You'll always be close to my heart, dear. Now I had better get to my story before I doze off. That happens to us senior citizens earlier than we like to admit."

"Trust me," I say. "Dozing off early isn't confined to the senior set. My family teases me about not being able to make it through a movie that starts after seven o'clock."

"Well then, for both our sakes, I'll try to be brief." Aunt Bette pours a cup of tea. "Lucy, I'm not sure if you knew this, but I haven't lived in Tredway my entire life."

"Actually, I wasn't aware of that until I read the note you left for me at Locust Hill. I just assumed . . ."

"Of course you would, dear. The truth is, I was somewhat of a rebel for a woman of my day. My parents expected me to marry and settle down . . . preferably nearby. But I would have none of it. The thought of spending my life in small-town Nebraska was about as appealing as a wart on my thumb."

We all chuckle.

"Really? What did you want to do?" I can't help but ask.

"I had my sights set on becoming a fashion designer in the clothing capital of the world — Paris. Although World War I had ended several years before, things were still unstable in Europe. I didn't want to cause my parents unnecessary worry. They were already opposed to my leaving Nebraska. It took some convincing, but they eventually agreed to allow me to attend the Stanley Fashion Institute in New York City."

"Aunt Bette, I had no idea!" Lucy leans forward.

"How could you? All this occurred long before you were born, my dear."

"It must have been exciting to live in New York," I say. "What was it like back then?"

"Oh, my dear!" Aunt Bette laughs. "You make it sound like ancient history!"

"I'm so sorry. I didn't mean to . . ."

"No, no offense taken, dear. It *was* quite a long time ago. More than seventy years now. Gracious! How time flies!"

I grin in an effort to contain my embarrassment.

"Now to answer your question, dear. New York was very cosmopolitan, of course. I loved everything about it — the theater, restaurants, design school . . . even the pulse of the city. I thought I had found the life I was born to live."

"So what brought you back to Tredway?" asks Kelly.

"The same thing that often brings a woman back to the security of her family — a broken heart."

"Oh, I'm so sorry, Aunt Bette."

"Don't be, Kelly dear. I've come to understand that God often allows difficulties for our own good. This period in my life was no exception. The only problem was that I didn't realize it at the time. I came back to Tredway a very bitter woman."

"Bitter? I can't imagine it!" says Lucy.

"I'm afraid it's true." Aunt Bette gazes out the window at the black night. "The memory of those dark days is still fresh in my mind . . . Anyway," she continues, returning from her reverie, "I decided to stay on in the city after design school. I accepted a job with an up-and-coming designer that was too good to refuse. For fifteen years I was his senior assistant."

I'm impressed. "You were quite the career woman."

"Definitely . . . and very independent. That is, until I met Walter."

"Walter?" asks Lucy, seeming a bit more relaxed.

"He was one of the photographers who covered our spring show for a local trade magazine. Although he arrived late, he was able to charm me into giving him backstage access. Afterward he insisted on returning the favor by taking me out to dinner."

"So he must have been handsome?" I ask.

"Liz, you are so shallow!" Kelly teases.

"Actually, he was quite handsome — at least in my eyes. But even more attractive was that Walter was unlike any man I had ever met. He was warm, witty, and full of adventure. I remember one time he surprised me with a picnic in Central Park . . . at midnight."

"Midnight in Central Park?" says Kelly. "I'd definitely call that adventurous."

"He kept me guessing. A few months later,

Walter asked me to marry him. I surprised everyone — including myself — by saying yes."

Lucy sighs. "How romantic."

"Oh yes, it was very romantic . . . and Mother and Father were thrilled. I think they were relieved that their independent daughter was ready to settle down. And once they met Walter, they loved him."

"It sounds just like a fairy tale," I say.

"Well, as I said, this fairy tale did not have a happy ending. These were the days before the Salk vaccine. Walter had the misfortune of contracting polio."

"How terrible for you, Aunt Bette." Lucy reaches to take her hand.

The old woman's eyes mist over. "Yes, it was terrible. My sweet Walter, who was so full of *joie de vivre,* was forced to spend his last days encased in one of those horrid iron lungs."

"You mean one of those long, steel machines?" Kelly asks. "Where you could only see the person's head?"

"Exactly. And I'll never forget the sound it made — *whooshing* in and out to expand his lungs just so he could breathe. I sat by his bed day and night, praying he would recover and we could continue with our wedding plans. I watched him suffer for two months before he finally gave in to the disease. I was shattered."

"Oh, Aunt Bette," Lucy whispers, "I'm so sorry."

"Thank you, dear." She pats Lucy's hand. "I had a lot of support from my friends and family, but I could not understand how God had allowed this to happen. How could He take away the man I loved before we even started our life together? It didn't seem fair. After Walter's funeral I quit my job and came home to Tredway. I didn't have the energy — or the desire — to do anything else. I spent a lot of time in my room.

"The years passed, and I worked at a dress shop in town. After Mother and Father died, I found myself alone at Locust Hill. I was like one of those ghosts that supposedly haunt the house. Just floating through life."

"By the way, how did that rumor about the ghosts get started?" I ask.

Kelly frowns. "Liz, don't change the subject."

"I just wondered."

"Actually, what I'm about to share with you is tied into those old stories."

I smirk at Kelly. "See? I wasn't changing the subject."

"Shush!" says Kelly. "Please go on, Aunt Bette."

"One day, as I was moving some furniture in my bedroom, I came across a loose floorboard. I pulled the board up to remove the old nails and repair it. Under the board I was shocked to find an old journal."

"A journal? Like a diary?" I asked. *This is getting good.*

"Yes. It was kept by my grandmother, Anna Simmons Crawford, when she was a girl."

"And it was hidden all those years?" says Lucy.

"Apparently so. I never heard Mother or Father mention it."

"So did you read it?" I ask.

Aunt Bette smiles at me. "Of course, dear. I was depressed — not dead."

I felt the heat of embarrassment creep up my neck.

"I'm just teasing you, dear." Amusement sparkles in her eyes. "Actually, I read the journal from cover to cover that same evening."

Lucy appears impatient. She hugs herself as if the room has suddenly turned cold, then finally says, a bit brusquely, "Aunt Bette, this has all been very interesting, but I'm still not sure what it has to do with my questions."

"I'm sorry, dear, but we seniors have a

tendency to run on and on, don't we?"

"I'm being rude again, aren't I?"

"No, you are quite right." The old woman laughs. "Now where was I?"

"You were going to tell us what Anna had written in her journal."

"No, I think that's something you need to read for yourself. Finding Anna's journal was a turning point in my life, and it came at a time I definitely needed to go in a new direction. Lucy, I'm sorry to make you and your friends listen to all this ancient history, but I think you'll find the answers you're seeking within the pages of Anna's journal. I also suspect you may discover the answer to questions you might not even realize you have. Just try to keep an open mind, dear."

"I guess that's the least I can do. Thank you, Aunt Bette."

"I've lived a long time, and there's one thing I know to be true. Learn everything you can from the bumps in the road. That way you may not have to bounce over them again." She smiles kindly. "As you read Anna's journal, think about the reasons God may have brought you to Tredway, and remember His promise to guide you over the rough spots."

Aunt Bette takes Lucy's hands in her own and gives them the gentle squeeze of reassurance that can only be passed from one who has traveled the same road.

"Now, where has young Emma disappeared to? I'll ask her to fetch the journal from my room so you ladies can be on your way."

As we walk to M.A.'s SUV, a piece of paper flutters from the tattered brown leather journal Lucy has tucked under her arm.

"Oh, look!" Lucy points to the paper blowing down the drive.

"I'll get it," I volunteer, running ahead and trapping the slip of paper under my shoe. I pick up the rose-colored sheet and hand it to Lucy. She sobs quietly, then reads aloud what Aunt Bette had written:

And we know that God causes all
things to work together for good to
those who love God, to those who are
called according to His purpose.
ROMANS 8:28

■ ■ ■ ■

CHAPTER TWELVE

■ ■ ■ ■

Liz's Triple Chocolate Pecan Brownies

1 package brownie mix
1/2 cup white chocolate chips
1/2 cup semisweet or milk chocolate chips
1/2 cup coarsely chopped pecans

Instructions

1. Preheat oven to 350 degrees.
2. Prepare brownie mix as directed on package. Add remaining ingredients to batter.
3. Put batter in greased 9×9-inch pan. Bake 40–45 minutes until toothpick inserted near center comes out clean.

Before Jeff left Locust Hill, he built us a cozy fire in the front parlor to take the chill off the fall evening. As I settled into one of the old armchairs, I found it surprisingly comfortable. My prior experience with antique furniture has consisted of a painful afternoon perched on the edge of a sofa to avoid a loose spring.

I suspected it might be a long night, so I set up an assortment of soothing herbal teas and a tray of my specialty, Triple Chocolate Pecan Brownies, on a small walnut table near the couch, within easy reach of all of us. My motto is, "When life gets sticky, dip it in chocolate."

Jess walks into the room. "Liz, this looks wonderful. You definitely overstated your lack of domestic ability in your last column."

"You better watch out, kiddo, or we'll be back to calling you Martha," Marina adds as she settles cross-legged on the old sofa.

"No chance." I lift my chin in determination. "Just as your fence-hopping days are over, I've turned in my pastry bag and spring form pan."

"So how are your readers taking this change of attitude?" Kelly, who has claimed the other armchair, is already methodically picking the pecans from her brownie.

"It's hard to believe, but I've only had a

handful of negative e-mails. Apparently most of my readers feel the same way I do, but were afraid to admit it. Many of them wrote that they can't wait to see the changes."

"Have you decided on your first topic?" asks Jess.

"I interviewed this lady in Omaha who can make a dozen freezer meals in a couple of hours."

"Twelve meals in two hours? I want her phone number!" Marina exclaims.

"Speaking of phone numbers," teases Lucy, who has just walked in the room with Mary Alice, "did Jeff ask for yours?"

Marina rolls her eyes. "Oh yeah . . . right after I called him a tree hugger."

"Seriously, Marina," says Jess, "I noticed a few sparks flying between you two this afternoon."

"That's called *friction,* Jess." But two spots of red dot Marina's cheeks like she's a life-size Raggedy Ann doll. "Can we change the subject? Please?"

As Lucy and Mary Alice sit down on the edge of the hearth with their desserts, Jess pulls out the journal. "So, are we ready to begin? And you're sure you want me to read, Lucy?"

Lucy nods, and Mary Alice takes her hand.

"I guess I'll start at the beginning." Jess turns the brittle, yellowed page to the first entry.

■ ■ ■ ■

CHAPTER THIRTEEN

■ ■ ■ ■

Pioneer Mush

3 cups water
1 teaspoon salt
1 cup cornmeal
Additional sugar or syrup

Instructions

1. Bring water and salt to a rolling boil.
2. Add cornmeal. Turn heat to low — or cook over another pot of water (double boiler).
3. Simmer 20 minutes, stirring often.
4. Serve immediately with sugar or syrup.

February 14, 1861

It is St. Valentine's Day, and I am in a sour mood. Mother and Papa were in a gay mood all day — teasing and exchanging playful looks. Rather than being infectious, their foolishness has created the opposite effect. It has drawn me into an even darker mood. How can they appear so happy living in this infernal wilderness, where each morning brings a sad reminder of our distasteful circumstances?

Fourteen-year-old Anna Simmons woke to the pelting of icy rain against the sides of the rough log cabin. In an effort to avoid the cold wind drifting through the chinks in the wood, she huddled lower in the feather tick.

It looks like another lovely day on the prairie, I wonder how many times I'll slip on the ice on the way to the barn this morning. Yesterday it was four times. Maybe today I'll only fall twice.

The sound of her mother's voice from the room below shook Anna from her thoughts. "You've slept long enough, child. I need you to draw water. And your father will be needing help in the barn."

"I'll be down in a moment, Mother," replied Anna, pulling the worn quilt over her head once again.

I hate it here! I hate all of it, lamented Anna silently. *I hate the cold, the wind, the mud — even the coarse people who have moved into town. Why would Mother ever agree to leave our family and friends in Ohio to settle in this wild Nebraska Territory?*

"Anna, are you coming? I need your help," called Emily Simmons sharply.

"I'm sorry, Mother. I have to find my stockings."

"Be quick, child." Her mother peered over the railing of the loft to check on her daughter's progress. "We are expecting visitors again this evening, and in this weather, they will be worn out."

"Yes, Mother."

Visitors, thought Anna, *always visitors. The only news that could add more unpleasantness to this day is to find that our new house on Locust Hill has burned down while we slept, forcing us to live in this drafty cabin another two years. Maybe if we had fewer visitors, Papa would have more time to finish our house.*

Almost immediately Anna felt the familiar pang of guilt for her uncharitable attitude. One couldn't help but feel sorry for the fugitives — travel-worn, sick, hungry, frightened — who found their way to their cabin. But Anna also worried. The seemingly endless train of

237

refugees had almost depleted the family's meager supply of food. Food that had to last them through the remainder of the cruel Nebraska winter.

The fugitives were also often in dire need of clothing to replace their rags. And they always needed shoes. Anna could not believe how many arrived barefoot, even in the midst of a Nebraska winter. It was a heart-wrenching sight. She shivered just thinking about it. But how much was one family expected to do?

Anna dressed quickly and descended the stick ladder that connected her sleeping loft to the kitchen. Her mother already had a cheerful fire going in the hearth. Emily's small frame was bent over the fire, stirring the pot of mush she had prepared for breakfast.

A long homespun apron covered her woolen work dress. Her honey-colored curls were twisted into a bun at the nape of her neck. She turned at the sound of her daughter's footsteps on the wood plank floor. "There you are, sleepyhead."

Anna was relieved that the sharp tone was gone from her mother's voice. Now amusement lit her sapphire eyes upon seeing her still-sleep-rumpled daughter. "You'll need your cape, dear," she advised. "The weather is wicked this morning."

"I heard ice on the roof," Anna replied. "I

hope this doesn't mean another blizzard is on the way."

"We will just have to pray against that possibility. Travel is dangerous enough without a blizzard complicating things."

Anna fastened the hooded wrap at her throat and grabbed the wooden pail by the door. "I'll draw your water first, Mother. Then I'll help Papa with Buttercup."

"Thank you, dear. You don't have to come back in. Just leave the water by the door."

Anna braced herself for an icy blast of prairie wind and then flung open the door to the cabin. The harsh prairie gusts buffeted her slim frame as she made her way to the well behind the cabin.

Yes, she thought, *I despise this place . . .*

The cold wind continued to blow all day. And just as I suspected, snow is beginning to pile up on our doorstep.

I chose to retire to my loft as Mother and Papa await the arrival of our visitors. Out of necessity I am making this entry in secret, my only light a flickering stub of a candle. Papa insists on complete silence regarding our activities, warning that discovery will bring dire consequences. I once tried to confide in Mother, hoping for a sympathetic ear, but she has little patience for grumbling. Though I am forced to keep you hidden, dear diary, you are my cherished friend. For without you in which to pour out my heart, I would surely burst . . .

The fire in the Locust Hill front room has burned down to glowing embers. Marina gets up to put on another log as we discuss what Jess has just read.

"One thing's certain," Kelly announces. "Teenagers haven't changed much in the last 150 years. Anna sounds a lot like my Michaela."

"And my Katie," I add. "But I know my daughter wouldn't be caught dead in a cape. Did I tell you she went through my overnight bag to make sure I hadn't packed anything embarrassing to wear this weekend? I'm getting tired of being called a fashion emergency."

Marina nods. "I'm telling you . . . different era but same attitude."

"Let's be honest," says Jess. "How many of us would cheerfully go out in a blizzard to draw water from a well? Much less milk a cow?"

Marina looks puzzled. "I don't remember hearing anything about a cow."

"Who do you think Buttercup was, Rina?"

asks Jess.

"It could have been the cat."

We groan.

"Remember, I'm a city girl." Marina examines her meticulously painted red nails. "The only cows I've seen are on television. Or, now that I think of it, maybe at the zoo."

Mary Alice tactfully changes the subject. "Actually, I think it's kind of reassuring to know that teenagers were pretty much the same yesterday as they are today."

"It's hormones, ladies," states Kelly, "with a healthy dose of teenage stubbornness."

"I know," I add. "Jess keeps trying to convince me that the alien who's invaded my daughter's body will eventually move on to torment another unsuspecting family. I'm just hoping it doesn't move to Josh."

"Be strong, kiddo." Jess squeezes my shoulder. "Remember when I pasted one of Sarah's baby pictures inside the kitchen cabinet? It was to help me remember that there was a core of sweetness in the midst of all that" — she puts her hands on her hips and wiggles her shoulders for effect — *"attitude."*

"That's why you did that? But, Jess, Sarah is such a sweetheart —"

"Of course she is . . . to you," interrupts Marina. "All our kids are nice to other adults. It's when they get us alone that the trouble starts."

"Maybe it's a teenage plot designed to keep parents on the edge of sanity. Willing to turn over the car keys at the drop of a hat," I suggest.

"OK, ladies," says Kelly, "I think we've had enough conspiracy theory. How about getting back to Anna's journal?"

"Would you like me to go on, Lucy?" Jess asks.

The five of us turn to face Lucy. She is huddled on the hearth — knees clasped to her chest — rocking almost imperceptibly. I realize she hasn't uttered a word since Jess began reading Anna's journal. There's a pained expression on her face as she slowly opens her eyes.

"Aren't any of you wondering who these visitors are that Anna refers to? I mean, in light of what Jeff and Marina pulled from behind the wall, these people could be —"

"Stop right there, Luce," Marina orders in her tough-cop voice. "We all agreed to collect the facts before making any assumptions."

Lucy's voice is tiny. "I know but —"

"But nothing," Kelly interrupts. "A deal's a deal. Keep reading, Jess."

"Lucy?" asks Jess.

"Fine." Lucy's jaw stiffens. "But don't say I didn't warn you. This could be a lot worse than any horror novel. In this story the characters are real."

We are quiet as Jess turns the page.

"It looks like the next entry is almost eight months later . . ."

■ ■ ■ ■

CHAPTER FOURTEEN

■ ■ ■ ■

Corn Pudding

1 cup corn (fresh or frozen)
1 egg
1 cup light cream
1 tablespoon salt
1 tablespoon sugar
1 tablespoon butter

Instructions

1. Place corn in bowl. Add egg and beat together.
2. Add cream, salt, and sugar.
3. Melt butter in the baking dish.
4. Pour corn mixture into hot baking dish and bake at 350 degrees for 30 minutes, or until brown on top.

October 16, 1861

The knock on our back door came just before first light. Earlier in the week, Papa had received word that we could expect visitors at Locust Hill. What none of us expected was the dreadful sight that lay behind the door . . .

Anna Simmons dressed in the dark, silently thanking God for her new woolen stockings. A hard autumn frost had arrived last week, leaving a sharp chill in its wake. Although it was Sunday, Anna's mother had instructed her to put on her work dress and apron. She would change into her "almost new" Sunday dress and bonnet after receiving their visitors.

As Anna laced her boots in the upstairs bedroom of their new house on Locust Hill, she heard a series of soft thuds, followed by her mother's sharp gasp. *What in the world?* Anna thought, racing down the staircase and rounding the corner to the kitchen.

The room was cast in a series of shadows. Anna's parents, Joseph and Emily Simmons, had risen earlier to cover the windows in anticipation of their visitors. The only light in the kitchen glowed from their new cast-iron stove. In the dimness Anna saw her mother bent over what appeared to be a form heaped in the doorway.

"Quick — help me get her in here," Joseph ordered a man outside the door. "Then you can hide the wagon and the others in the barn."

"Please be careful with the poor dear," said Emily, smoothing the unconscious woman's hair away from her face as the two men carried her body across the threshold.

"Good, you're up, child," Joseph told Anna after turning to see her in the doorway. "Spread a quilt near the stove so I can get a look at her."

A careful physician, Joseph bent down and gathered the young woman in his arms like a newborn. When Anna had the quilt ready, he placed his patient facedown on the makeshift pallet. In the flickering light, Anna saw that the back of the woman's thin dress was in shreds — and crusted with a brown substance that appeared to be blood.

"The barbarians," muttered Joseph. "Emily, you'll need to cut away these rags so I can dress the wounds. I'll prepare a poultice."

Checking often to be sure the woman was still breathing, Joseph spent the next hour carefully cleaning her wounds.

The scene was too much for Anna to bear. "Papa, may I bring food and water to our visitors in the barn?"

"In a moment, child, but first fetch my smelling salts. I want to try to rouse her. She needs to get some water down. Just from her cracked lips, I'd wager she hasn't had any food or water for several days."

"Joseph, why don't you let me try," suggested Emily. "The poor thing is apt to be frightened out of her wits if you're the first face she sees upon waking. That's not to say that you aren't handsome . . . just a bit imposing."

"You make a good point, as always, Mrs. Simmons," Joseph replied, giving his wife an appreciative hug. "Anna, let's see what needs to be attended to in the barn."

"The sun is up," said Emily. "Perhaps you should hide the food in the water pail so as not to attract attention if someone happens to be passing by."

In the barn Anna distributed fresh milk and the corn pudding her mother had prepared the prior evening for their hungry guests. Two men and four women were huddled in the straw the driver had spread on the dirt floor. Their tattered clothing and haggard faces spoke of a difficult journey — and the hard life that preceded it.

As Anna worked, she overheard her father ask how the young woman was injured. She cringed as the driver related the sad tale of a brutal beating at the hand of a slave owner.

"You see, suh, ol' Massa died last month

and Young Massa take over. He a hard drinker, even though his mama cry her eyes out over it. He have his eye on Mary there ever since she a young girl in the quarters.

"Mary, she done got permission las' year from the Ol' Massa to marry a fine fella over on another plantation. She birthed her first lil' baby 'bout a month ago. A right cute thing, if I do say so myself.

"Well, Young Massa don' like his people thinkin' they married. He say a slave got no right to be married . . . so he tries to get Mary to come stay wid him in the big house. Mary says she don' wanna stay wid him coz she married. Young Massa been drinkin' and gets powerful angry. He tells her to wait in the yard.

"Po' Mary waits there all day and all night. In the mornin' Young Massa comes out and says, 'Now then, do you want to stay wid me in the house, or you want to live in the yard like a dog?'

"Mary, she a good girl . . . right religious. She say, 'Massa, I married. It's not right I stay in the house wid you. I have a young-un.'

"Well, this puts Young Massa in a hateful mood, and he say, 'Well then, you can live like a dog.' So he has Ol' Jake chain Mary to a stake set right in the ground. He say she has to eat and drink out of a bucket jus' like a dog.

"Well, Mary jus' sits there in the sun all day. Young Massa leaves her chained to that stake for two more days with jus' water one time a day. Now Mary's startin' to feel poorly wid no food and jus' a little water, so Young Massa thinks he got her broke.

"He comes out and stands over Mary and say, 'Now are you ready to do what I say? Or do you want to die like a dog too?' Mary jus' opens her eyes and looks at him, sayin' nothin'. Then, all of a sudden, she sits up and spits right on his boot.

"Well, suh, this makes Young Massa so powerful mad that he hauls off and kicks her right in the face with his big ol' boot. Then he tells Ol' Jake to fetch his bullwhip.

"Suh, I never seen nothin' like it. He tore that po' girl up and then left her in the yard — still tied. Even Ol' Jake, who seen a lot of things, couldn't tolerate what Young Massa done."

Joseph looks at the dusty barn floor, shaking his head.

"Some folks in the quarters know I is a conductor and I be leavin' that very night. So they wait till Young Massa sleepin' off his whiskey. Then they unchain young Mary and carry her to where we be waitin'.

"I almost said no to takin' her coz she hurt so bad. I don' think she make it. But I jus' couldn't leave that po' child behind, so I hide her under the sacks with the rest of the folks.

"We been on the road three nights 'fore I know 'bout a station where we can stop . . . and Mary be havin' a hard time of it. Many a time I think she already dead. But I come to find she breathin', so we keep on.

"Suh, that girl been through a powerful hard time, but she tough. I know it a lot to ask, but I think she needs doctorin' for a spell before she can go on."

Joseph looks up at the man.

"I don' want to burden your family, but I gots to go on with these folks come dark. I sure 'preciate if you could let Mary rest here for a while. I be comin' back in a week or so to take her on down the road."

After the conductor finished his tale, Joseph stared at his hands for several minutes, as if not knowing what to say. Anna came to her father's side and rested a hand on his shoulder. He looked up at his daughter, a sad smile softening the sharp planes of his face.

"Mary will remain here with my family until she is fit to travel," said Joseph, his voice full of determination. "You and your people rest here today. I'll send word to the next station to expect you before dawn tomorrow."

"Thank you, suh. May the dear Lord bless you and your family for your kindness."

"Come on, Anna," said Joseph, rising from the rough bench he and his daughter had built from a downed cottonwood. "Let's see what we can do to help your mother in the house. Then we need to dress for morning services. We don't want to attract attention by missing Reverend Lemmerman's message."

Mother, feigning ill, stayed with Mary while Papa and I attended morning services. I know Papa is a capable doctor, but I am not sure his skill is sufficient for this task. If this young woman is to live, it will only be by the grace of God . . .

"I feel like such a fool," says Lucy, jerking us back into the twenty-first century.

"Luce, I keep telling you," Marina orders. "Quit making assumptions before we have all the facts. You're beginning to grate on my nerves . . . just like one of the rookies I have to deal with each day. Gimme a break!"

"I'm sorry, Marina, but it's like a huge weight is being lifted from my shoulders. I'm beginning to think my family members may not be the monsters I thought. In fact —"

"See?" Marina interrupts. "That's exactly what I mean. *Rookies!*"

"Rina, how about a little patience with us

rookies?" says Jess kindly. "I, for one, would like to hear more from Anna's journal. How about the rest of you?"

"Please, Jess, go on," I encourage while Kelly and Mary Alice nod their agreement.

"Yes, please," Lucy joins in. "The story is just beginning to catch my interest."

CHAPTER FIFTEEN

SICKBED SOUP

1 large chicken
1 white turnip, peeled and cut into chunks
1 yellow onion, cut into chunks
2 parsnips, peeled and cut into slices
1 sweet potato, peeled and cut into chunks
3 carrots, peeled and sliced
5 pieces of fresh dill (if available)

Instructions

1. Put everything into the pot with about 3–4 quarts of water. Make sure chicken is covered.
2. Simmer until chicken can be easily removed from bones and vegetables are tender.
3. Debone chicken and return meat to soup.

October 17, 1861

I have never been so frightened! Poor Mary lay prostrate in our kitchen, barely clinging to life, when I heard the unmistakable sound of approaching danger . . .

As Anna worked in the garden, gathering the last of the fall vegetables, she heard the creak of wheels and the *clomp* of horses, indicating that a wagon was making its way up to Locust Hill. She immediately put down her basket and ran to the edge of their small orchard to inform her father that visitors were on the way.

She needn't have bothered, for Joseph had apparently also heard the wagon and was striding toward the house. Having provided shelter for fugitives in the past, the Simmons family was well aware of the importance of keeping their activities secret.

Putting a finger to his lips, Joseph quickly spanned the gap between himself and his daughter. "Anna," Joseph whispered, "go into the house and help your mother move our guest to the safe room."

"But, Papa," Anna protested, "you said yourself Mary shouldn't budge until —"

"It can't be helped. Now do as I say, child!"

Feeling the sting of her father's reprimand, Anna hurried into the kitchen through the back door. A large built-in cupboard was already standing open — providing access to the tiny room built in the wall behind it. Anna's mother was nowhere in sight.

"Mother?" Anna whispered hoarsely. The young woman on the makeshift bed stirred.

"Anna!" answered Emily, slipping quietly from the darkened space behind the cupboard. "Quick — help me get Mary over here."

Through the open windows, Anna could hear her father's friendly greeting.

"Hello, Mrs. Olsen! Matthew! What a surprise! To what do we owe the pleasure of your company at Locust Hill this fine afternoon?" boomed Joseph in his deep baritone.

Anna let out a deep sigh of relief at her father's words. Their visitors were friends of the family. She had feared the wagon might contain a slave owner or one of his detectives searching for the fugitives.

"Hurry, child! We don't have much time! I've spread some quilts on the floor of the room for Mary to lie down on."

"But, Mother, it's only Mrs. Olsen and Matthew. Surely it's not necessary —"

"Anna, this is no time to argue with me. I'll explain later. But now I need your help!"

Supporting the young woman on each side, mother and daughter half walked and half carried the injured slave across the kitchen floor.

"I loathe having to do this to you, dear," Emily whispered to the barely conscious woman. "But, for your safety and ours, we can't take a chance someone will betray us. Remember, Mary, you must remain absolutely silent until we come for you. Do you understand?"

Her face twisted in pain, the young woman weakly nodded her assent.

Just as the women reached the opening to the hiding place with the frightened fugitive, Emily stiffened.

"What's wrong, Mother?"

"Listen," she said, inclining her head. "That surely couldn't be the wagon leaving, could it?" Before Anna had the opportunity to reply, she heard the creak of the front door and the familiar sound of her father's step in the front hall.

"Papa?" called Anna.

"Yes, it's me. And, gratefully, I'm alone." Joseph stepped into the kitchen, carrying a cast-iron kettle. He placed it on the stove and quickly crossed the room to help his wife and daughter with Mary.

"The Olsens are gone?" asked Emily, as she and her husband gently led the young woman back to the cot.

"Yes, but unfortunately, I had to enter into a bit of deception to accomplish it."

Emily supported Mary as she carefully lowered herself to the cot. Anna helped her father slide the cupboard back into place, once again successfully concealing the tiny room.

"Well, Joseph, do tell," said Emily as she handed a cup of water to Mary. "What is this bit of deception you passed on to dear Audrey Olsen?"

"Mrs. Olsen was understandably concerned about your health after learning that you had missed Sunday services."

"So this must be her famous Sickbed Soup," said Emily, lifting the lid from the kettle Joseph had placed on the stove. The heady scent of chicken and fresh vegetables filled the kitchen. "Audrey is such a dear and, I might add, a gifted cook."

"She is a kind soul," agreed Joseph, "and sorely wanted to check on you. I told her I hadn't reached a firm diagnosis, and there was a chance you might be contagious."

"Oh, Papa!" exclaimed Anna. "You didn't!"

"I did. But as I said, I truly hated to deceive her."

"Don't worry, dear. I'll visit the Olsens in a day or two to put Audrey's mind at ease . . . and extol the healing properties of her recipe."

"Well, Mrs. Olsen's soup will be just the thing to help you regain your strength, Mary," said Joseph, bending down to check his patient's progress. "Do you think you might be able to take a few sips?"

The young woman offered a nod and weak smile in reply.

"Yes," said Emily, putting the soup on the rear of the stove to warm, "the Lord always provides, doesn't he?"

Mother is right — the Lord always provides. But in this case, I wish His provision would have arrived with a bit less drama. Later Papa and I talked about why we couldn't let the Olsens in on the secret. With so many of the fugitives' lives at stake, and our own, too, Papa says the fewer that know, the better.

"And I thought there was a lot of drama in *my* life," Marina states. "Cops have nothing on these guys."

"Speaking of your chosen profession," says Lucy, "can we start putting the pieces together?"

"Whaddaya mean? It's obvious. The Simmons were helping fugitive slaves. The space behind the wall was built as an emergency hideout. Case closed."

"Thank you, Inspector Holmes," I tease.

"So this whole rookie thing was just a ruse so you could solve the mystery yourself," Kelly reasons before Marina grasps the playful dig in my comment. "Figures, Favazza."

"Wrongo once again, Kelly Belly. You, too, Lizzie. You guys have got to realize that some things are better left to the professionals. Trust me; in the long run, I saved you a lot of headaches."

"You are hopeless!" Kelly says, shaking her head.

"I know, and that's why you all love me so much."

After a round of indignant groaning, eye rolling, and a shower of balled-up napkins, Lucy brings us back to the subject at hand. "So Joseph and Emily Simmons were abolitionists. All the way out here in Nebraska. That possibility didn't even occur to me when we found that room."

"It sounds like they may have been part of the Underground Railroad," Jess guesses. "That would explain the chains and manacles. They probably came from fugitive slaves. They would have to keep them hidden in case their home was searched."

Marina frowns. "Without a warrant? I don't think so."

"When it came to conflict between abolitionists and the proponents of slavery, civil rights didn't mean a whole lot."

"So, Jess, tell us," says Kelly. "Which child

did a report on this subject? You know way too much for having just a casual interest."

"Actually, all the kids did a unit on the Civil War and the conflict over slavery. But the Underground Railroad really caught Sarah's interest. She chose it as the topic for a research paper last spring. I can't wait to tell her that Locust Hill may have been a station."

"Station?" asks Mary Alice. "I didn't think the Underground Railroad was a real railroad."

"It wasn't, but it functioned much like one," explains Jess. "Fugitive slaves were referred to as freight. Conductors were those who escorted them — either on foot, in wagons, or by boat. And safe houses along the escape route, like Locust Hill, were called stations. Joseph would have been the stationmaster."

"So how come Locust Hill isn't listed in the National Register of Historic Places — or something like that — as one of these stations?" asks Kelly.

"The system was shrouded in mystery," Jess continues, "even after the war. Many people never revealed their roles in the railroad. It was a difficult time in our history."

"For the pro-slavery people, hearing

people talk about the railroad after the war was probably like rubbing salt in old wounds," says Lucy. "Even though you had different beliefs, they were still your neighbors."

"Makes sense," I admit, "but I have another question. From what I've read, the Simmons were a religious family, right?"

Kelly nods. "They must have been, to start a Christian college in the middle of nowhere."

"OK, so if they were so religious, how did they justify lying to the authorities? I mean, I know slavery was wrong, but . . ."

"Lizzie, you and Sarah think a lot alike," says Jess. "That was the thesis for her paper."

"Great, Jess! I'm just a hairsbreadth from menopause and still think like a teenager."

"A very perceptive teenager with a Christian worldview," adds Jess. "Not that I mean to brag . . ."

"Go ahead, brag," I say. "Sarah's a great kid."

"We're waiting," pipes up Marina. "What did she come up with?"

"Sarah compared the actions of those involved in the Underground Railroad to three instances in the Bible where God's people deceived an unjust authority for the greater good."

"Very good," says Kelly, obviously impressed. "Did she get an A?"

"You decide after I tell you what she came up with."

Jess explained that Sarah used the account of two midwives in the book of Exodus who deceived Pharaoh to circumvent an unjust order. Pharaoh felt the captive Jewish nation was becoming too strong, so he ordered the midwives to kill all the baby boys born to Jewish women. The midwives decided not to carry out the order, and their deception allowed the birth of Moses.

"So the end justifies the means?" asks Marina. "I'm not sure I buy that."

"No, that's not what she concluded," insists Jess. "Sarah also used the example of Rahab, found in the book of Joshua."

"I've always liked that name," I say. "Ray-hab. It has a nice ring to it."

Kelly grimaces. "Focus, Liz."

"Actually, Kelly, I am very familiar with the story of Miss Rahab. She was a . . . how shall I put this delicately . . . ?"

"She was a hooker," Marina pronounces, "who protected the Israeli spies from being ratted out to the authorities. What I'd like to know is, what were the Israelites doing at her house in the first place?"

"Liz, you and Marina are just like my kids." Jess laughs. "Always trying to get me to go down a rabbit trail."

Marina and I look at each other sheepishly.

"Does this mean detention?" I ask.

"Can we *please* get back to the subject?" There's more than a hint of exasperation in Kelly's voice.

"OK, I'm sorry. I promise to be good."

"What's the bottom line, Jess?" asks Kelly. "What did Sarah conclude?"

"Actually, I thought it was quite good. She brought the issue to the present day in the case of Judge Roy Moore."

"Wasn't he the chief justice in Alabama who wouldn't allow a monument with the Ten Commandments to be removed from the courthouse?" I ask.

"That's the one," says Jess.

"I remember seeing something about that on the news," Mary Alice comments. "There was a big protest as troopers carried off the monument."

"Yes, and Judge Moore ended up being removed from office," says Jess.

Marina combs through her wild black hair with her fingers. "So how does this tie in with lying to authorities?"

"Sarah argued in her paper that all these

269

examples had to do with nonviolent civil disobedience."

"I'm afraid I'm lost," Lucy admits.

"You have to remember this is from a fifteen-year-old kid," says Jess, "but I think she made some pretty good points."

I smile. "Said like a true mom."

Jess smiles back.

"Granted. But Sarah had the facts to back up her stand. She said the Bible teaches us to honor and obey our government. But when the government places a demand contrary to the Word of God, Christians must respectfully decline to obey. That's called civil disobedience."

"OK, I understand how this applies to the midwives and the abolitionists," says Kelly, "but I'm still a little foggy on the Alabama situation."

"I was too," Jess explains, "but Sarah did her homework. She quoted a former Reagan cabinet member who compared Moore's fight to the moral battle to get rid of slavery and segregation. He said the federal court had distorted the meaning of the Constitution in regard to the separation of church and state, and Christians were obligated to take a stand against the court's ruling."

"And that's just what Judge Moore did," I

conclude.

"And so did Joseph and Emily," whispers Lucy, almost to herself.

"I can see Sarah arguing before the Supreme Court, Jessie," Mary Alice says.

"You are such a sweetheart, M.A." Jess looks as pleased as a mother cat. "You never know."

"Now that we all have a grasp on the concept of civil disobedience," says Kelly, "how about getting back to Anna's journal?"

"Your wish is my command." Jess turns the page to the next entry.

■ ■ ■ ■

CHAPTER SIXTEEN

■ ■ ■ ■

Green Tomato Pie

Pastry for a two-crust pie
3 cups sliced green tomatoes
1 1/3 cups sugar
3 tablespoons flour
1/4 teaspoon salt
6 tablespoons lemon juice
4 teaspoons grated lemon rind
3 tablespoons butter, cut up

Instructions

1. Line an 8- or 9-inch pie pan with crust.
2. Combine tomatoes, sugar, flour, salt, lemon juice, and rind in a bowl. Spoon into pastry shell. Dot with butter.
3. Cover pie with top crust, seal edges, and make several slits in the top of pie.

4. Bake at 450 degrees for 10 minutes. Reduce oven temperature to 350 degrees and bake 30 minutes more.

Note: Pioneer kitchens would often substitute vinegar for lemon juice. Cooks lucky enough to have spices might also add cinnamon, allspice, and cloves.

October 26, 1861

Mary appears to grow stronger each day in both body and soul. I must admit, it wasn't until this morning that I had much hope for her. She had been terribly distraught when her fever broke to discover the conductor had left her baby behind. I heard Mother tell Papa that she feared Mary might recover physically, only to die of a broken heart.

After church services this morning, Papa told us he intends to set out for Missouri this afternoon to rescue Mary's daughter.

October 28, 1861

Papa arrived home just before dawn with Mary's baby girl wrapped securely inside his overcoat. Mary wept and kept touching the baby's face, as if she couldn't believe she was real. It is truly a miracle, and I am so proud of Papa. To celebrate, Mother prepared a special dinner — including Papa's favorite, Green Tomato Pie.

For the first time, Mary had enough strength to join Anna and her parents at the table for dinner. This was also a first for another reason. Earlier, as she had rocked and caressed her baby, Mary had shyly confided to Anna that dinner would be the first time she would be sitting down to eat with white people.

Mary explained that, unlike his son, her former master was generally a kindly man and treated his slaves well. However, he and his wife maintained strict boundaries with their servants. Any slave who presumed too much "familiarity" with a member of the family would face very unpleasant consequences. Mary told Anna that she would never have been allowed to eat with the family as she was invited to do in the Simmons household.

So it was with much hesitation that Mary sat down at the table that evening.

After offering the mealtime prayer, Joseph said, "Mary, it seems my wife and daughter have been taking good care of you in my stead. How are you feeling?"

Apparently too timid to speak, the young woman didn't look up from her dinner plate.

"Go ahead, dear," Emily prompted. "You can answer. My husband is not nearly as gruff as he appears."

"Gruff?" Joseph laughed. "You must be mistaken, my dear. I am as gentle as Anna's tabby kitten. The one she calls Precious."

"Papa, have you seen how Precious pounces on the mice in our fields?" teased Anna. "I'm not sure 'gentle' is a fitting description."

Mary seemed to relax in the midst of the

family's casual bantering.

"Sir, it's not that I'm scared of you," said Mary, timidly entering the conversation. "I'm just not used to white folks talkin' to me like a proper person."

Emily's eyes clouded. "Oh, my dear child."

Joseph put down his fork and folded his hands before speaking. "Mary, you know more than most people that this is not a perfect world. In fact, parts of it are profoundly evil. But, child, you must learn the truth and stand on it. The Good Book tells us that all people — both black and white — are created in God's very image and are equal in His sight."

"That's very true, dear." Emily gently took the young woman's hand.

"Many years ago," continued Joseph, "I committed a verse to memory from the Good Book. It says: 'There is neither Jew nor Greek, there is neither bond nor free, there is neither male nor female: for ye are all one in Christ Jesus.' "

Tears began to slip silently down Mary's face as she listened to Joseph's words.

"During times of weakness or indecision, I draw strength from God's Word," Joseph continued. "It's my prayer that you will do the same, for the Bible also says, 'Hold fast to the truth and the truth will set you free.' "

I will miss Mary and her baby when they leave. It has been much like what I imagine having a big sister is like. But Papa has arranged for a conductor to stop for her any day now. As much as I would like her to stay, I realize it is not safe for her and the baby — or for us. Mother has assured me that one day — in this world or the next — we will meet again. Until then, we have much work to do.

Kelly sniffs as Jess stops reading.

"Pass the brownies," she moans, "and the tissues. I'm not sure how much of this I'm going to be able to take."

"What's that you always say, Liz?" Mary Alice teases. " 'When life gets sticky —' "

"Yeah, yeah," interrupts Marina, " 'dip it in chocolate.' So keep those brownies coming this way, girls."

"I'm so impressed with Joseph's commitment," says Jess.

"To ride into a slave state . . . not knowing a soul." I stop, humbled by his courage and determination. "He risked everything to rescue the child of a woman he barely knew. That's true heroism."

"I have to admit, the guy had guts," Marina allows. "I can tell he's one of your relatives, Luce."

"What in the world are you talking about, Marina? I jump at my own shadow these days."

"Face it, Luce. You're the only one with enough guts to stand up to me." She glares defiantly around the circle — apparently daring us to disagree.

I knew better than to take the bait. "You've got a point there, Rina."

"Got that right, Lizzie. But don't you others get any ideas, or I'll squash you like bugs."

"That's something to look forward to." Jess laughs. "But right now, I need a chocolate fix — and a soft pillow. I want to be alert when we finish Anna's journal."

■ ■ ■ ■

CHAPTER SEVENTEEN

■ ■ ■ ■

Hotdish

1 lb. very lean ground beef
1 can cream of mushroom soup
1 (15 oz.) jar of Cheez Whiz
1 (1/2 lb.) bag of Tater Tots

Instructions

1. Press raw hamburger evenly into the bottom of an ungreased 9×13-inch pan.
2. Spread cream of mushroom soup over hamburger.
3. Spread Cheez Whiz over the soup. Arrange Tater Tots over the top.
4. Bake in a preheated oven at 350 degrees for 1 hour and 15 minutes.

Janelle's Banana Split Cake

1 yellow cake mix
1 (12 oz.) can sweetened condensed milk

1 cup crushed pineapple, drained
5 bananas
1 (16 oz.) carton whipped topping
1 small package chopped nuts (toasted)
Maraschino cherries
Hot fudge or chocolate syrup

Instructions

1. Mix and bake cake mix according to instructions on package using a 13×9-inch pan.
2. While cake is warm, poke 12–14 holes in the top with the handle of a wooden spoon. Pour sweetened condensed milk over cake. Chill until cool.
3. When cake is cool, spread pineapple on top of cake.
4. Slice 5 bananas and arrange in layer over pineapple.
5. Use whipped topping for next layer.
6. Sprinkle with nuts, and top with cherries. Refrigerate overnight.
7. Before serving, drizzle top with hot fudge or chocolate syrup.

LAYERED SALAD

1 head lettuce, torn into bite-sized pieces
1 cup red, yellow, or green pepper, diced

4 hard-boiled eggs, cut in wedges
1/4 cup green onions, sliced
2 cups sliced mushrooms
1 carton cherry or grape tomatoes, halved
1 (10 oz.) package frozen peas, thawed
2 cups salad dressing or mayonnaise
2 cups cheddar cheese, shredded
8 strips of bacon, cooked and crumbled

Instructions

1. In a clear glass bowl, layer the first seven ingredients in the order given; do not toss.
2. Spread salad dressing or mayonnaise over top. Sprinkle with cheese and bacon.
3. Cover and refrigerate for several hours or overnight.

The sun is barely up when Marina tries to pull my feet from under the covers of the soft featherbed at Locust Hill. "Come on, Lizzie. It's a beautiful day."

"Go away." I put the pillow over my head. "I am *not* getting up."

My exercise-addicted roommate has been trying unsuccessfully to coax me from this delicious bed to join her on a morning run. This time I am determined to hold my ground — or, in this case, my bed.

"I promise to take it slow," she continues. "We'll just stay at an easy jog and enjoy the scenery."

Right! I remember the last time I was pressured to get out of bed at the crack of dawn by a fitness fanatic. Amber put even Marina to shame . . .

The sun had just peeked over the horizon as I stumbled out onto the porch with my sneakers untied. My early-morning coffee had already dribbled down the front of my new workout attire.

"There you are!" said the perky blond, jogging in place on my sidewalk. "I was beginning to worry you might have overslept."

Amber is a native Southern Californian. She and her family had recently relocated to Nebraska due to her husband's job transfer. She is sweet, energetic — and has upper arms that don't jiggle.

I knew there was something very different about Amber when she put my basket of "Welcome to the Neighborhood" blueberry muffins in a cupboard without taking even an appreciatory whiff. Before I left her clutter-free kitchen, she had convinced me to "walk" with her the next morning.

"I thought we were supposed to meet at 6:15," I mumbled. "My watch says 6:10. Or at least I think that's what it says. My eyes aren't fully focused yet."

"I thought you'd know I meant that we would *start walking* at 6:15," she chirped. "We have to warm up and stretch first. I was here just before 6:00."

"Sorry. This is all a little new to me. In fact, I don't think I've gotten up this early since I was breast-feeding Hannah. And then I kept my eyes closed."

"No problem, Liz! There's still time for a great workout!"

"Good," I muttered, silently thinking the exact opposite.

"By the way, I found an extra set of wrist and ankle weights for you." She handed me four bright blue objects resembling mini sandbags. "I'll help you strap them on. It'll really intensify your workout."

"I'm not in very good shape," I protested as she began to fasten weights around my ankles with Velcro bindings.

"Don't worry, that's the beauty of these things. You walk at your own pace and still get a killer workout!"

"If you're sure . . ."

"Hey, no pain, no gain, right?" she said, flashing perfect white teeth.

"Uhh, I guess."

"You're all set! Let's go!"

I knew I was in trouble when she charged up the hill in the classic form of a power-walker — elbows and knees pumping furiously. Less than a quarter mile into our walk, I began to feel the burn. After a half mile, there was an inferno raging in my arms and upper thighs.

"Amber," I gasped, bending over, hands on my knees, "could we slow down a little bit? I'm getting a little winded."

"If we don't keep up the pace, our heart rates will go down," she said, again jogging in place.

I tried to tell her that was the point. I *wanted* my heart rate to go down. In fact, my entire body was screaming to SIT down, but I was too winded to utter a word.

After a minute or two, I mustered enough

strength to push on. After all, I was representing our community to a newcomer. I didn't want her to think she had moved to the land of couch potatoes — even though, at that moment, I would have given anything to collapse on the closest sofa.

As Amber chattered on about vitamins and the newest phytonutrients, I tried to figure out a graceful way to ditch the weights that were torturing my extremities and crawl back home. I settled on the foolproof excuse available to all mothers — "The kids need me."

It took several minutes of surreptitious finagling until I was able to sound the ringer on the cell phone in my pocket.

"Oh! That sounds like mine," I gasped, snapping open my cell phone. "It must be the kids."

"No problem," replied my energetic partner. "I'll wait. I can do some lunges to tighten up my glutes."

Having no idea what a glute was, I smiled and put the phone to my ear.

"Hannah, is that you, sweetheart?" I asked the silent phone. "No, don't cry, sweetie. Just tell me what's wrong."

I paused for effect.

"Poster board? You need yellow poster board for a project at school TODAY. Well, honey, I'm right in the middle of my work-out, but I guess I'll have to cut it short. I'll be right home." I snapped the phone shut, shaking my head. "That was Hannah. A school-supply emergency. I'm going to have to run to the store to pick up some poster board. Kids! It's always something, isn't it?"

"No problem, dude, I've got you covered," she replied, still jogging in place.

Did she just call me "dude"?

"My daughter Mandy has a whole pack of poster board. We can stop by the house after our walk."

"But yellow . . . she certainly doesn't have yellow, does she?" I stammered.

"Of course. That's the best color for signs."

As I looked at the formerly innocuous neighborhood street before me — now looming like the side of a mountain — I realized I had to think quickly.

"Markers!" I shouted. "Hannah also needs SCENTED markers. The kind with glitter in them."

"Sorry, can't help you there." She turned and jogged up the hill. "Six tomorrow morning?"

"I'll call you," I shouted after her. "I may have a conflict."

As I ripped the Velcro to free my ankles, I

muttered, "A conflict with these infernal weights . . ."

Just the thought of the week of physical agony I endured following my walk with Amber gives me the resolve to resist Marina this morning.

"No way. No how. You might as well give up now, Marina, because I am not leaving this bed."

"Your loss, kiddo." She bounds from the room.

Maybe. But maybe not. I happily turn over in Aunt Bette's old four poster bed.

A couple of hours later, after setting out a simple breakfast of coffee, juice, and bagels, I am drafted to help Kelly hang the grass cloth Mary Alice has picked out for the library walls.

"This is such a great space." Mary Alice's eyes scan the small book-filled room appreciatively. "I think the light-colored grass cloth will help keep the cozy feeling but still open it up. What do you think?"

"To be perfectly frank, M.A.," I say, "all I'm thinking about is how in the world we're going to hang this stuff."

"Actually, it's the same as wallpaper, but the grass cloth isn't prepasted. You'll need to apply the glue by hand."

I raise an eyebrow. "How in the world do we do that?"

"Obviously, we brush it on." Kelly picks up the large brush on top of the bucket of wallpaper paste. "Looks easy enough."

"You're right, Kelly," Mary Alice agrees, appearing anxious to move on to a more interesting project. "That's all there is to it. Just make sure you coat the paper well."

"Gotcha."

"I know how to snap a chalk line," I offer, not wanting to seem totally DIY (do-it-yourself) challenged. After all, I had the DIY network programmed in our cable-channel lineup.

I learned this trick from my quirky college roommate who was a bit of a fussbudget. She was very particular about having her own space, so once a week she would snap a chalk line to divide our room in half. I've always longed to snap one of those buggers myself.

"Then I think we've got it covered," says Kelly. "No pun intended."

"Lucy and I will be in the kitchen installing the tiles I painted for a backsplash," Mary Alice explains. "Let me know if you need anything."

"By the way, M.A.," I say before she is

out of earshot, "I love those tiles. You know I'm going to hit you up to do some for me when we finish up with this project."

A blush creeps up Mary Alice's neck. "It's just a simple pattern. You could do it easily."

"Doesn't she read my column?" I mutter as she walks down the hall.

When I turn around, I see that Kelly has already begun to apply paste to the grass cloth. "Kel, shouldn't we measure how long of a piece we need first?"

"If you want to," she says with a hint of annoyance. "I thought we could just estimate once we get the paste on."

The last thing I am going to do is argue with Kelly about the best way to hang wallpaper — a subject I know nothing about. So I decide to get started on my chalk line. After attaching the top of the chalk to the crown molding, I drop the string and secure it with my index finger where it has dropped. All that's left is the fun part. A snap of the string, and I have a perfect chalk line on the wall.

Kelly applauds. "Way to go, girl. We'll have this up before lunch."

Once we have what Kelly thinks is a sufficient length of grass cloth coated with the gooey wallpaper paste, I ask, "So, what's the next step?"

"Why are you asking me?" My friend picks up one end of the sticky wallpaper and gestures for me to do the same. "You're the wallpaper expert."

"What are you talking about?" I say while trying to keep the floppy paper from folding over and sticking together. "I've never hung wallpaper."

"You've never hung wallpaper!" she exclaims. "What was all this 'I can do the chalk line' stuff? I assumed you knew what you were talking about."

"I did . . . do . . . know what I'm talking about," I retort. "The chalk line is perfect."

She wrinkles her nose in exasperation. "What good is knowing how to do a chalk line if you don't know how to hang wallpaper? People don't go around putting chalk on their walls for no reason."

"For your information, there are lots of projects that require a chalk line."

"Such as?" Clearly Kelly's unwilling to concede the point.

"Lots of things."

"I'm waiting." Still holding her sticky end of the grass cloth, Kelly begins to tap her toe.

By now, the sheet has begun to wrinkle in the center and stick together.

"Kelly, this is no time to argue. We have to get this stuff on the wall."

"Fine," she says, starting up the ladder. "It can't be that hard."

"Wait! I'm taller. Shouldn't I do the top?"

"For goodness' sake, the ladder is six feet tall. I can do it. Just follow my lead."

For some reason, this is not reassuring. As Kelly tries to line the top edge of the grass cloth under the crown molding that caps the walls of the room, she smears my chalk line.

"Stop!" I shout. "You're erasing the chalk line!"

"So what? What do we need a chalk line for anyway?"

"I'm not sure, but I know it's important."

Four hours — and a wallpapering manual — later, we have successfully applied two strips of grass cloth to the library walls.

"I'm ready for a break," says Kelly. "We can finish this up after lunch. By the way, what are you cooking, Liz?"

I shove my sticky hands into my pockets to keep from doing something I'll regret.

After ridding my hands of wallpaper paste, I decide to see how Jess and Marina are coming along with the landscaping before preparing lunch. Jess has planned a garden of perennials to bloom throughout the growing season. She has already put in beds of sunny coreopsis, dusty pink coneflowers, winsome daisies, and a pair of fragrant dwarf lilac bushes to border both the front and back steps.

"Doesn't look like much now," says Jessie, looking up at me on the front porch, "but fall is the perfect time to put in perennials. It gives the roots time to develop."

"So, when will these bloom?" I ask.

"The lilacs will bloom in early spring, but the rest should produce flowers most of the summer."

"I can't wait to see it next year."

"Actually, we probably won't see much. Perennials take time to establish. I remember my grandmother telling me the first year the plants sleep. The next year they creep. And the following year they leap. The leaping is what makes a gardener's work worthwhile."

"Sleep. Creep. Leap. Easy enough to remember — even for me. Where's Marina?"

"She's been putting in bulbs along the front walk and driveway. I'll say one thing . . . once she gets going, that girl has energy." Jess grins.

"If only it would kick in at a reasonable

hour." I sigh. "I might have to bunk with the more athletically challenged tonight and let Rina have the room to herself."

"Did I hear my name?" Marina strides around the corner of the house carrying a trowel and a basket of bulbs.

"Jess was just telling me what a great job you're doing with the planting. Lucy will be so surprised in the spring."

"I think I'm actually beginning to enjoy digging in the dirt. It's relaxing. If it wasn't so hard on my manicure, I'd be tempted to try it at home. Oh well, such is life."

A loud, grating noise draws our attention to the street. Jeff is attempting to back a trailer loaded with a construction Dumpster up the narrow gravel drive. The trailer hitch, which has dipped on the steep drive, is scraping against the ground. The load is shifting perilously.

"Hey!" shouts Marina, charging toward the truck. "Be careful there, Bubba! I just spent the last four hours planting bulbs, and you better not touch a single root on their hairy little heads."

"Well, my friend, if you call me Bubba one more time, I will be forced to file a complaint citing a hostile work environment."

Marina rolls her eyes.

"Seriously, how about helping me guide this thing up the drive? You do know how to direct traffic, don't you, girlie?"

"Talk about hostile working environments!" she teases.

"So what do you think, Jess?" I ask as we watch Marina help Jeff maneuver the Dumpster into place. "Is that love in the air?"

Jess smiles.

Both satisfied the Dumpster is positioned correctly, Jeff and Marina join Jessie and me on the porch for a glass of mint iced tea.

Marina takes a long swig. "Good tea, Liz. I love mint."

"I do too. I found a patch of it out back. I was surprised it was still there. I didn't see any other herbs."

"Mint is one of those plants that multiplies like fireflies on a summer night," says Jess from her seat on the porch swing. "Once you plant it, it's yours for life."

"What in the world . . . ?" I point to the caravan of cars heading up toward Locust Hill.

"Liz, I thought we had this conversation," begins Marina.

"Stop while you are ahead, my dear," I fire back. "I've had my fill of razzing from

Kelly this morning. I will say what I please."

"Well done, Lizzie." Marina laughs. "That backbone is beginning to poke through that preppie turtleneck after all."

I give her a wry smile.

The caravan of cars turned out to be a contingent from Aunt Bette's Ladies' Guild at Tredway Community Church.

"Thought you might need a little sustenance," says Janelle, the first to step from her vehicle with a covered dish. Apparently she's the leader of the pack. "Seein' how you've been workin' so hard up here."

I feel a huge smile creep across my face. I silently thank God for small favors — and country cooks.

Before we knew it, the efficient church ladies had set up our midday feast in the sunny kitchen and were on their way out the door. They wouldn't even consider our invitation to join us, implying with much head wagging and finger shaking that they didn't want to keep us from our work. *Too bad,* I thought. *I — at least — could use a break!*

After the Tredway ladies had waved goodbye, climbed back into their cars, and headed back down the driveway, looking like a trio of bumper cars, we didn't waste any time. Within minutes all six of us were digging into the hearty home-cooked meal, anchored by a delicious casserole one of the church ladies had referred to as hotdish. When I'd mentioned to Janelle that I had never heard of hotdish, she explained that the cook was from Minnesota.

"I never could understand why Minnesotans have to go and confuse things," she had said. "Why can't they call a casserole a casserole? Anybody in her right mind knows the dish is gonna be hot."

At least Janelle couldn't complain about the name of the salad. It was exactly as it looked: Layered Salad. Now there's a no-nonsense recipe title, and it tasted as good as it looked. I couldn't help myself. I had seconds.

Since we are all a little worn out from our morning projects, we decide to eat our dessert — Janelle's Banana Split Cake — on the sunny front porch. I'm curled up in the old-fashioned porch swing with my shoes off, the sun warming my back, and the decadent dessert filling my bowl. My friends are sprawled on nearby cushions and chairs as we enjoy the companionable silence that comes from years of shared experience. If this were heaven, I would be happy.

"The sun feels so good." Lucy stretches lazily in a chaise lounge. "I could sit here all afternoon."

"How about if we kick back and hear a little more from Anna?" Marina suggests. "We can get back to work in a couple of hours."

"Are you up to more reading, Jess?" asks Kelly.

"I think you can twist my arm." She rises to get the journal from inside the house.

■ ■ ■ ■

CHAPTER EIGHTEEN

■ ■ ■ ■

JOHNNYCAKES

1 cup cornmeal
2 tablespoons flour
1 tablespoon sugar
1/2 teaspoon salt
1 1/2 tablespoons shortening
1 cup milk
1 egg, separated

Instructions

1. Sprinkle cornmeal and flour into a cake pan and lightly toast (about 5 minutes) in 400-degree oven.
2. Mix toasted cornmeal, flour, sugar, and salt in a bowl.
3. Add shortening and hot milk.
4. Beat egg white until stiff. Fold yolk into beaten white. Finally, fold in corn mixture to the egg batter.
5. Drop batter from spoon into an

oiled pan, leaving space in-between cakes.

6. Bake at 400 degrees until golden brown.

April 24, 1862

There will be no sleep for me tonight. I am in a state of great agitation due to my own cowardice and selfishness! The only remedy I can fathom is to confess my depravity to God and to you, my secret confidant. This afternoon, while I helped Papa prepare our old buckboard for another errand this evening, I implored him to reconsider his role in the Railroad . . .

Juggling a covered basket and several large quilts, Anna made her way to the barn. The sun was just beginning to set, casting a golden glow over the prairie. She knocked sharply three times on the weathered barn door — a prearranged signal to her father. She heard the scrape of the latch as he unlocked the door, then slid it open just wide enough for her to slip in.

"Papa, I brought the johnnycakes Mother baked for your errand this evening," she said, blinking to adjust her eyes to the dimness in the cavernous barn.

"Thank you, child." Joseph relieved her of the bundle of quilts. "Your sewing circle has been busy. God will reward you for those sore fingers someday!"

Anna set the basket of food on the bed of the wagon, carefully wedging it between two jugs of water. She turned back to look at her father, who was spreading a thick layer of fresh straw on the bottom of the wagon.

"Anna, help me cover the straw with your lovely quilts, will you?" he said. "We want our guests to be as comfortable as possible on what promises to be a bumpy ride tonight. Only the Lord knows how much they've been through to get this far."

As Anna worked with her father to put the finishing touches on the preparations, her brow furrowed with indecision. She was still uncertain about broaching what would surely be a difficult subject. Finally, she glanced up from her task to find her father looking at her quizzically.

"Anna, you seem troubled. Is there something I can help you with?"

"I am troubled, Papa," she admitted, "but I'm afraid bringing up my concerns may upset you."

"Child, you know I care deeply for you. I'll do whatever is in my power to put your fears to rest."

"That's just it, Papa. Your activities are the source of my fear. How can you continue your work on the Underground Railroad when you know it is so dangerous?"

Joseph took a deep breath and turned from his daughter. "Anna, I thought you understood why we have opened our home to the fugitives that come our way."

"But, Papa, I read a notice posted in Mr. Meyer's shop when I was in town yesterday. It calls for the return of the fugitives — the ones who are resting in our kitchen this very moment — to their owner in Missouri. It even offers a hundred-dollar reward to the man who does so."

Joseph turned to face his daughter. "Anna, haven't I taught you that no man can own another?"

"Of course, Papa. But not everyone sees things as you do. Sheriff Blatt is being pressured by some of our own neighbors to enforce the Fugitive Slave Act and —"

His eyes narrowed. "That is a hateful law, child. Completely unjust."

"But, Papa, it is the law. Susan told me at services last week that the Hall County sheriff put a farmer in jail for allowing a family of fugitives to sleep in his barn. He also has to pay a thousand-dollar fine or lose his property."

"Do you know this man's name, Anna? Perhaps we can help —"

"Oh, Papa! Don't you see?" Anna cried. "I don't *want* you to help anymore! I'm frightened for your safety! What if Sheriff Blatt takes you to prison? How will Mother and I survive in this place without your protection?"

"Anna, dear child — ," Joseph began.

Anna cut him off. "I know these poor souls need our help. But, Papa, it's against the law to help them. Doesn't the Bible teach that we are to obey the laws of our land?"

"Immoral laws cannot be obeyed, Anna," he said, his voice full of conviction, "and they will not be obeyed by me. If I am arrested for doing my best to obey the teachings of the Bible, then let me go to jail. Our lives are in God's hands, and I feel I have His approval."

"But Papa, the notice said the fugitives had committed terrible crimes and those who helped them would be considered accomplices."

"Anna, I suspect the only 'crime' these brave souls committed was to escape from the tyranny of an unjust system that has kept them in bondage all of their lives. But, regardless, do you think the Good Samaritan stopped to ask whether the man who fell among the thieves was guilty of any crime before he helped him? If you came across a poor woman who had fallen into a ditch, would you have to be satisfied she was not a criminal before offering your help?"

"Of course not, Papa, but the risk right now . . ."

"I cannot — and will not — let fear keep me from doing what I know is right . . . what I

312

have known is right since the time I was a boy."

As I blathered on and on like a scared kitten, Papa put down his bundle and motioned for me to sit with him. He paused several minutes before speaking. During the silence, I was quite uncomfortable, anticipating a stern lecture regarding my lack of moral rectitude. Instead, when Papa turned to me, he seemed to be in great turmoil . . .

"My dear child," Joseph began, "it has always been my hope and prayer that this day would never come. I do all I can — just as any father would — to shield you from the evil in the world." He bowed his head. "I see I can no longer do so."

Anna sat with rapt attention as her father related an incident he had witnessed as a young man. An incident he firmly believed God used to fire his hatred of slavery.

"I was still living with my parents in North Carolina. Although I was familiar with slavery, we owned no slaves ourselves and had very little contact with those who did.

"On this particular day, my father had asked me to deliver some tools in need of repair to the blacksmith shop near our farm. When I reached my destination, I saw that the black-smith was riveting a chain around the neck and wrists of a slave. All the while the poor man's master chastised him for running away. Their conversation is as seared in my mind as if the blacksmith had touched me with his poker.

" 'Didn't I treat you well?' asked the slave owner.

" 'Yes, Massa,' replied the frightened young man.

" 'Then what made you run away?'

" 'My wife and young-uns were taken away from me because you refused to sell me with 'em. I think as much of my family as you do of yours — as any white man does of his. When I saw 'em taken, I had to follow.'

"Anna, words can't convey the despair in the man's voice or how his body trembled. It was enough to melt all but a heart of stone, which is, apparently, what the slave owner's chest contained.

"The cruel man totally disregarded this father's desperate plight and continued to press him to reveal those who had helped him escape the plantation. When the brave young man refused to betray those who had be-friended him, the master laid the slave's shackled hand on the blacksmith's anvil and struck it with the hammer until blood seeped from the fingernails. The man winced with each cruel blow but remained silent.

"The slave owner then became enraged with the man's refusal to speak and ordered the end of the chain, which was riveted to the man's neck, to be attached to the axle of his buggy. Once this was complete, the owner took off at a fast trot, forcing the slave to run at full speed or be dragged along the ground by his neck."

Anna's father turned to her and added quietly, "I watched them until they disappeared down the road. For as long as I could see, the slave was running.

"As I stood in the road, a strong hatred for oppression and injustice welled up in me. As a boy I was helpless to intervene in what I knew was a sin against God and humanity. I vowed that when I became a man, I would not sit by idly and allow this evil to destroy our great nation."

Joseph took his daughter's hand and looked straight in her eyes. "Ever since that day, I have thought of that slave. I have prayed he was able to keep running behind that buggy. That he was able to stay alive . . . until someday he could escape and live his life as a freeman, as God intended."

Papa and I resumed our work in silence

— he firm in his resolve and me distraught over my selfishness. No, there will be no sleep for me tonight.

"Shall I go on?" Jessie asks. She gently closes the journal on a finger to mark her place.

But there are no voices — no sound — except for the lonely call of a loon in the distance.

■ ■ ■ ■

CHAPTER NINETEEN

■ ■ ■ ■

Totally Decadent Hot Fudge Sauce

1/3 cup butter
4 oz. unsweetened chocolate
2/3 cup boiling water
2 cups sugar
1/4 cup corn syrup
1 1/2 teaspoons vanilla

Instructions

1. Melt butter in a 3-quart pan over low heat.
2. Add chocolate; stirring, until melted.
3. Stir in water, sugar, and corn syrup.
4. Bring to a boil over medium heat and cook without stirring until sauce is thickened and glossy, about 7–8 minutes.
5. Stir in vanilla.

For what seems like a long time, none of us on that front porch in Tredway speak. Each woman is apparently lost in her own thoughts. Just listening to Anna's account of man's inhumanity to a fellow human being is disturbing. Not just on the surface, but way down deep. Much like reading a news story about a gruesome murder and finding out it happened on the next block.

I also wonder if a part of my discomfort stems not just from the slave owner's behavior, but my own if I were to witness a similar scene. Joseph Simmons showed tremendous courage, never wavering from the course he knew was right. He backed up his words with action.

Would I, Elizabeth Harris — a woman who often has trouble even standing up for her political beliefs — do the same in the face of such danger? Would I be willing to risk everything to help people I didn't know and would likely never see again? All because it's the right thing to do?

Evidently I'm not the only one thinking this way.

"Joseph Simmons really bucked the system," Kelly says. "Opening his home to all those fugitives could have gotten him in big trouble."

"Maybe it did," I add. "We don't know

the end of the story yet."

"I can imagine making some quilts, like Anna did, to keep the runaway slaves warm. Or feeding them dinner, as Anna's mother did," Mary Alice murmurs. "But would I do more?" She focuses on her hands, clasped in her lap. "I'm not sure I could dare take the risk. Especially if it meant my family might get hurt . . ."

"Or you might end up in jail," Kelly states.

"It would take a lot of guts," I admit. "No wonder Anna was scared. I'd be scared, too — for myself and my family."

"Just think how frightened the slaves were. Separated from their families. Treated more like animals than human beings." Jessie pauses. "Actually treated worse than animals, like that young slave who had to endure so much."

Lucy's eyes look sad and misty. "How could someone be so cruel?"

Marina flexes her fists. "I'd want a few words *alone* with that slave owner. Some fightin' words. The kind of guy I'd like to knock into tomorrow."

"All that poor man wanted was to be with his family," Lucy continues. She takes a shaky breath. "Don't we all want the same thing? To be with the ones we love?"

Again, quiet descends.

I think of Lucy, who has recently lost two of the people she loved the most. Of Marina, who never planned on divorce . . . or being a single mom. Of the young slave and his family, who were separated by the cruelty of a slave owner and the unjust "law of the land."

Then I think of how much I have, and I'm ashamed of ever complaining.

Marina finally breaks our heavy silence. "I feel like the kid who didn't study for the history test, but I've never heard of the Fugitive Slave Act. I thought Nebraska was a free state."

"Jess," says Kelly. "What'd this law have to do with Nebraska? You have a library of history texts at home."

"Hey, kiddo, I have menopause knocking at my door. Just wait and see what it does to your short-term memory."

"Stop it, Jess," I plead. "I get a hot flash just thinking about menopause. And I'm wearing a turtleneck today."

"Lizzie, you are way too young to be worried about menopause," says Lucy.

"Maybe, but I'm very susceptible to suggestion."

Jessie chuckles. "You're a stitch, Liz! Seriously, all I know about the Fugitive Slave Law is that it was designed to prevent abolitionists from helping slaves who had run away from their owners. I don't remember the particulars."

"Wait one minute!" All of a sudden Mary Alice pops up from her chair and hurries into the house.

"Where do you think she's going?" asks Kelly.

"Beats me," I say, "but please pass that hot fudge sauce Janelle left with her dessert. I hear chocolate prevents hot flashes."

Face flushed, Mary Alice rejoins us on the porch. Clearly she's excited about something. "Craig gave me this new cell phone for my birthday. It connects to the Internet."

Lucy shakes her head. "Now I really feel out of touch. I never knew such a thing existed."

"Me neither, until I got it. You know how Craig loves gadgets. I hate to admit it, but I thought he bought the phone more for him than me."

"Typical," says Marina. "One time Bobby bought me a year's subscription to satellite TV for Christmas. It had sixty-four sports channels."

"Actually, Craig must know me better than I know myself because now that I know how to use it, I'm addicted. It's so convenient."

"For what?" says Kelly. "Why would you need to surf the Net in your car?"

"I've used it to look up movie times, restaurant hours — even our bank balance. And one time I downloaded a map to Claire's soccer game when I couldn't find the field."

"Now *that* would be handy. Unlike Kelly, who has a natural sense of direction" — I look at her and grin — "I am always getting lost."

"Very funny," says Kelly. "Maybe there's a spot for you on *Last Comic Standing* after all."

"Play nice, girls," Jess warns.

"So, M.A., show me how this thing works." Marina moves closer to look over her shoulder.

"See? I used the keypad to type in Fugitive Slave Act. Now I just hit Send. The phone connects to the Internet and runs a search."

"Phat," says Marina.

"Phat?" I ask. "Rina, did you say *phat?*"

"Liz, phat means —"

"I *know* what it means. My kids told me that *phat* means 'cool,' not 'fat.' But I still can't help looking at my thighs every time I hear it. I vote to add it to the list of words banned from FAC conversation."

"Only if we can also ban 'low carb.' "

"Deal," I say.

Marina and I shake hands to seal our agreement.

"Here it is . . . the top-five matches," Mary Alice reports. "Now I just select the one I want to pull up."

"Let me see." Kelly cranes her neck, apparently changing her mind about the usefulness of Mary Alice's high-tech phone.

"Technology is amazing," says Jess. "I just wish it came as easily to me as it does to my kids."

"Here we go," Mary Alice adds. "I have an article about the Fugitive Slave Act from a U.S. history site."

"What does it say?" I ask. "Can you read it to us?"

"Well, it looks like the law was passed in 1850 in return for Southern support of California's admission to the Union as a free state. And you were right, Jessie, the law was designed to help slave owners protect their property."

"It is so sad to hear people referred to as property," says Jess.

"I know what you mean," Marina chimes in. "One of my elementary-school field trips was to the old courthouse in St. Louis where the *Dred Scott* case was argued."

"The case sounds familiar but help me out," I ask.

"From what I remember, Dred Scott was a slave who sued for his and his wife's freedom after their owner died. The Supreme Court ended up ruling that black people could never be citizens and had no right to sue."

"The Court also said Congress couldn't pass a law to outlaw slavery," says Jess.

"You're kidding? That came from the U.S. Supreme Court?" Kelly's tapping her toe again.

"Makes you understand how *Roe v. Wade* came about," adds Jess, shaking her head.

"Does it say how the law was enforced, M.A.?" asks Marina.

"Let me scroll down. Here it is. I'll read it. 'The new law created a force of federal commissioners who were empowered to pursue fugitive slaves in any state and return them to their owners. These slave catchers, as they were called, received ten dollars for each man, woman, or child they seized. No statute of limitations applied — therefore slaves who had been free for many years could be returned.' "

"That's heartbreaking," Lucy declares.

"Just think how many families must have been torn apart."

"It says here that the commissioners could force local citizens to help them apprehend runaways. And if a person refused, they were arrested and fined."

"So if you were arrested for not helping to hunt down a runaway slave," says Marina, "what was the penalty?"

"Pretty stiff, if this article is right," Mary Alice explains. "It says the fine could be as high as a thousand dollars, along with six months in jail."

"I understand now why Anna kept her diary hidden, even when the Civil War was over," says Lucy. "Even after slavery was abolished, there were probably some people who would not have agreed with their decision to participate in the Underground Railroad."

Jess turns to the next page of the journal. "From what we've seen so far, her entries aren't very regular. The next one is almost four months later . . ."

■ ■ ■ ■

CHAPTER TWENTY

■ ■ ■ ■

Griddlecakes

2 cups cornmeal
1 teaspoon salt
2 tablespoons sugar
2 cups boiling water
1 cup milk

Instructions

1. In a pan, mix cornmeal, salt, and sugar.
2. Stir in boiling water and milk.
3. Drop 1/4 cup batter on hot, well-greased griddle. Cook on both sides until golden brown.

August 10, 1862

There was a soft knock in the middle of the night, which usually means an unexpected stop. I've come to recognize Papa's step as he hurries down the stairs to open the door . . .

The largest man Anna had ever seen was warming himself before the stove in the Simmons' kitchen. Even without his battered brown hat, he was almost a full head taller than her father — a man of significant height himself. His chest reminded her of a large barrel. His legs were like tree trunks.

Anna was so shocked at the sight that she was tempted to tiptoe back to her bedroom and fasten the latch on the door. She held her breath when the big man turned to face her, and her heart pounded in fear.

Then she saw his eyes — dark eyes full of kindness. His wide smile immediately dissolved her worries.

"Anna, I'd like you to meet our guest," Joseph said. "This is Mr. Miller. He goes by the name of Big Henry."

"Hello, Mr. Miller." Anna smiled. "It's nice to meet you."

"Nice to meet y'all too, missy," said the man with a twinkle in his eyes. "But I'd shore feel better if y'all called me Big Henry."

"Thank you very much. I'll do that, *Big Henry.*"

She grinned at him, and he grinned back, showing broad, white teeth that glistened even in the dim light of the kitchen.

"Anna, your mother is not feeling well," said Joseph. "Would you mind preparing some breakfast for our guest? He's come a long way, and I suspect he is quite hungry."

"Yes, Papa. Right away."

"That's mighty kind, missy," said Big Henry. Still gripping his hat in his hand, he nodded politely. "Thank you."

Anna set about putting together a hearty meal — all the time wondering how much food such a large man might eat. She mixed a double batch of griddle cakes and put a slab of salt pork on to fry. As she tended the skillet, Big Henry and her father continued to talk in hushed tones.

"We hadn't received word that you might be arriving, Henry," Joseph explained. "How did you know it was safe to stop here?"

"A fella I met down in Kansas Territory told me to look for the house on the hill. He said it safe if I see the quilt like the one he showed me hangin' on the line in back. I was a happy man to see that quilt!"

"Where did you come from, Henry?"

"Texas, suh. I run cattle for Ol' Massa since

I was a young-un. Before I was even born, my folks come to Texas with Ol' Massa from Missouri — 'round a town called Potosi. He came out wid Mister Stephen Austin to settle the Texas territory. My pappy fought right 'longside Ol' Austin in the war for independence.

"Las' year my folks took sick and passed on. Ol' Massa promised them he would set me free 'fore he died. After we bury my folks, he say to me, 'Well, here's your papers, Henry. You might as well go on now as later.' That's one thing 'bout Ol' Massa — he a man of his word."

"So you are a free man, Henry?" asked Joseph. "You have documents to prove this?"

"Yes, suh. They right here. Next to my heart." He patted his chest.

"Make sure you hang on to those papers," Joseph warned. "There are many unscrupulous people who would jump at the chance to try to sell you back into slavery."

"Don' I know it, suh."

"How did you make your way all the way to Nebraska?"

"I jus' followed the drinkin' gourd north. I walked at night so as not to cross any patty rollers who be lookin' for slaves that run away."

Anna heard her father's sharp intake of breath. "Henry, are you telling me that you walked here all the way from Texas by your-self?"

"Yes, suh. My pappy always say, soon as I get my papers, to go north to the promised land. He say Ol' Massa better 'n most to his slaves . . . but a man got to be free."

"I can certainly understand that, Henry. I am convinced the desire for freedom was planted in all men by our Creator."

"When I be runnin' cattle and sleepin' under the stars, I'd look up and think what it would be like to be free. I jus' couldn't get it out of my mind. No matter what people say, there no future for a slave."

Anna could hear the sadness in the man's words. She wondered if it was sadness for himself . . . or for those he had left behind . . . or maybe both.

"Well, Henry, you are no longer a slave. And your future is yours to do with as you see fit," Joseph declared. "Do you plan to go on to Canada?"

"Well, suh, I been ponderin' that. I'd like to go out West to see if I can get some work runnin' cattle. Maybe get some stock of my own. I'm pretty good with a horse and a rope — and I don' mind sleepin' under the stars. It helps a man remember the one that made him."

Joseph nodded. "You're right there."

"That's what I'd like to do. But lately I been thinkin' I might join up with the Yanks. I wanna have my own family someday, and I want my young-uns to know their pappy fought for freedom."

"Henry, I admire your courage," Joseph said slowly.

Anna could hear the hesitation in her father's voice.

"But you know there's a good chance you will be captured — or even die — if you choose this course," Joseph continued. "You've just tasted freedom. Are you sure you want to put it in jeopardy?"

"Well suh, that's what I've been ponderin'. What if all the Yanks . . . or old Mr. Lincoln . . . say it not worth riskin' their lives to stand up against the slave states that wants to keep things the way they is? Where would that leave me? Yep, I been thinkin' theys some things worth fightin' for."

The kitchen was silent as I served breakfast to Papa and Big Henry at our long table. It seemed both men were lost in their own thoughts. And so was I. For the first time since we moved to the Nebraska Territory and started working with the Underground Railroad, I am beginning to truly understand what freedom means —

and that keeping it has a cost.

"Lofty thoughts for a teenager," says Lucy.

Jess nods. "It's so easy to take freedom for granted when you're born with it. Anna saw that it isn't always a given."

"Makes you think, doesn't it?" adds Marina.

"I hate to change the subject, but now I feel like the one who didn't study for the history test," I apologize. "What's all this about following the drinking gourd?"

"I know this one," answers Jess. "The drinking gourd refers to the Big Dipper, which contains the North Star. Fugitive slaves used the star to keep them on the right course — going north."

"I was really interested in Anna's mention of a quilt used as a signal that it was safe to stop," says Lucy. "I remember seeing an episode of *Antiques Roadshow* that explained how different quilt patterns were used to communicate."

"I saw that same show," adds Mary Alice excitedly.

Marina rolls her eyes. "Figures."

"Quiet," I whisper, elbowing her playfully.

"Anyway," continues Mary Alice, "the log-cabin pattern meant it was safe to stop. Whereas the bear-track pattern meant a

337

runaway slave should hide in the woods and stay off the main road."

"I wonder if any of those old quilts are left," Jess muses.

"We should check the attic," Lucy suggests.

"Maybe later," Kelly insists, "but I'd like to find out what Big Henry decided to do. Keep reading, Jess."

■ ■ ■ ■

CHAPTER
TWENTY-ONE

■ ■ ■ ■

Emily's Potato Pudding

3 large potatoes, peeled
3 eggs, separated
1 cup granulated sugar
1/4 cup flour
1/2 teaspoon salt
1 cup cream
Sweetened berries, if desired, to serve with dish

Instructions

1. Boil, mash, and cool potatoes. Mix with egg yolks.
2. Beat egg whites and sugar until soft peaks form. Add this to potato mixture with flour, salt, and cream.
3. Bake at 350 degrees in a buttered 9×9-inch dish until firm, about 45–60 minutes.

September 10, 1862

Papa and Big Henry left today to enlist with Mr. Lincoln's Union forces. I am trying to be brave, but my deepest struggle is with bitterness. How could Papa leave Mother and me unprotected? Granted, before leaving, he took our good friends, the Olsens, into confidence regarding our work as a station on the Underground Railroad, as well as arranging for Matthew Olsen to live in the old cabin to help with the farm work. But he is just a boy — and an extremely shy one at that. About the only time he utters a word is to ask for a second helping of Mother's potato pudding. Papa says the war will be over soon. I am already counting the days until he returns!

Kelly tucks her feet underneath her and scoots around until she's more comfortable. "Once again, typical teenager. One minute spouting lofty ideals. The next minute 'It's all about me.' Not a thought about how difficult it must have been for Joseph to make this decision."

"Or that he may not come back at all," I add.

"With Joseph gone, I'm wondering about their work with the Underground Railroad," says Lucy. "If they were living alone, with only a boy to help out, it would be too dangerous to continue, don't you think?"

"There's only one way to find out." Jess turns the page . . .

CHAPTER TWENTY-TWO

EMILY'S CHICKEN AND DUMPLINGS

3 lb. chicken
1 medium onion, peeled and quartered
3–4 ribs of celery, cut in chunks
3 carrots, peeled and cut in chunks
1 sprig of fresh thyme
6 peppercorns
2 cups all-purpose flour
2/3 cup milk

Instructions

1. Place chicken in a 12-quart stock-pot.
2. Add onion, celery, carrots, parsley, thyme, peppercorns, and enough cold water to cover chicken. Simmer about 45 minutes or until chicken is falling off bones.
3. Remove chicken and debone when cool.

4. Strain stock and adjust seasoning.
5. To make dumplings: mix flour with milk to form a dough. Do not over-mix.
6. Drop dumplings into boiling chicken stock with spoon. Bring stock back to a boil, stirring often so dumplings don't stick together.
7. Cook 15 minutes until dumplings are done.
8. Return chicken to pot and serve.

November 3, 1862

I am so tired that my bones actually ache. We have had a steady stream of visitors all week. Thankfully, the Olsens have lessened the burden by taking in some of the fugitives. And Mrs. Olsen and her daughters are swift with a needle and thread. A true blessing, since most of the fugitives have arrived in rags — totally insufficient to continue on their journey north . . .

Anna's breath curled in little puffs in front of her face as she made her way to the smokehouse in the early morning light.

The Bible says that man cannot live on bread alone, she thought, *but even that sounds better than the squirrel and venison Mother has cooked for the last month.* Anna was grateful for the game Matthew brought back from his hunting trips — for they would starve without it. Nevertheless, how she longed for a pot of Mother's chicken and dumplings!

Once in the smokehouse, Anna pulled a stool across the floor so she could cut down the sack of meat hanging from the ceiling. This was their last ham. Mother had been saving it for when Papa and Big Henry came home on a furlough at Christmas. But both

Anna's and her mother's hearts had broken at the sight of the starving family that had arrived on their doorstep early that morning.

The young mother and her two children had been traveling with their owners across Missouri to join the Oregon Trail. A Confederate sympathizer, the farmer suffered great losses as a result of the war and thought he might have better luck starting over out West.

With food in short supply, the mother overheard the owner telling his wife it would be more expedient to leave the slave children to fend for themselves. The young mother pleaded with her master not to leave her children in the wilderness, but the cruel man refused to relent. Taking note of the young mother's distress, and fearing she might attempt to flee with her children, he chained her wrist to the covered wagon after setting up camp for the evening.

While the slave owner and his family slept, the young woman was able to work the hasp of the chain from the wagon and flee with her children.

That very morning, Anna's mother had discovered the terrified family hiding in their barn — the heavy chains still hanging from the young mother's wrist. As Locust Hill became known among conductors as a station on the Underground Railroad, discovering a group of fugitives who had stopped unex-pectedly had become a common occurrence.

At first Anna had been surprised by her mother's determination to continue participa-tion in the Railroad while her father was away at war.

"Mother," she had said, "surely Papa would not approve of continuing to accept visitors while he is away." Seeing her mother's deter-mined expression, she had added, "But per-haps we can help another way by providing clothing and other necessities."

"Anna, although we didn't speak of it, I am quite certain your father would prefer I not harbor fugitives at Locust Hill in his absence. However, child, I also know your father would realize this is a matter of conscience and would not deem to dictate mine."

"But Mother — ," Anna had begun to argue.

"I have prayed much about this, child," Em-ily said, "seeking to balance my responsibility as parent and citizen. But the Lord keeps drawing me back to the book of Deuteronomy, which says, 'Thou shalt not deliver unto his master the servant which is escaped from His master unto thee.' The Good Lord is plain in His teaching — and I cannot turn my back on it."

Anna knew from experience that it was use-less to argue with her mother. Once Emily

Simmons made a decision, there was no turning back.

So on this chilly morning, as she walked back to the house carrying their last ham, Anna remembered her mother's words and the fierce determination that backed them up — and steeled herself for another long, hard day.

Mother is hopeful a conductor will stop in the next day or so to escort the young family on its way to safety. I will include this request in my bedtime prayers, for now I am ready for some much-needed sleep.

"OK, now I feel guilty for criticizing Anna for complaining," says Kelly. "The poor kid has had to handle more in her young life than most people face in a lifetime."

"I find it hard to believe they actually continued operating a station on the Railroad," says Lucy. "They had to be scared to death."

Marina snorts. "These two chicks put any cop I know to shame. Keep reading, Jess."

November 4, 1862
Although quite exciting, today was a day I'd rather not repeat . . .

352

Anna woke to her mother's urgent whisper.

"Get up, child! We've got to hide our guests! Hurry!"

The sound of barking dogs and approaching hoofbeats jerked the young woman from her pleasant dreams to the reality of their present danger. Knowing instinctively there was no time to dress, she leapt from her warm bed in almost a single motion, grabbed her shawl from the peg, and ran to the kitchen.

Before the dying embers of the hearth, Anna saw the three slaves huddled together, rusty manacles still circling their wrists. Anna and Emily had tried for several hours to remove the primitive apparatus — with no success. In spite of the heavy chains, the young mother wrapped her thin arms around the children protectively. The six-year-old looked around the room with wide eyes as her younger brother began to whimper.

"Shush, Billy!" hissed the little girl. "We'll be all right if you just hush up! Ain't that right, Mama?"

In response, the mother gently ran a hand over the girl's braids and whispered to the toddler, "Hush now, baby. You stay close to Mama."

Working in the faint light, Emily yanked the few baskets and pieces of crockery from the cupboard shelves and struggled with the concealed latch. "There it is!" she exclaimed softly as the mechanism popped open. "Anna, help me with the door."

Through the wavy glass of the window, Anna could see the flicker of torches moving across the prairie as she and her mother managed to open the creaking cabinet.

At Anna's direction the young mother herded her children through the opening behind the cupboard and then disappeared into the dark space herself.

"Remember, not a sound," warned Emily, putting a finger to her lips. "Your lives depend on it!"

"Mother, what about a candle? It's so dark in there. The children — ," Anna began.

"There's no time," her mother replied, closing the secret panel. "Quick now! Put the dishes back into place while I fetch my nightcap. After all," she said, with a slight drawl and a coy smile, "we have to look like frightened gentlewomen — clearly unaccustomed to disturbances at this hour."

"I won't be acting, Mother. I'm shaking like a leaf!"

As Anna put the last dish on the shelf, Emily returned to the kitchen. Anna heard the coarse voices of several men dismounting from their horses. In a moment, they would be at the door.

"Be brave, child," said her mother, tying the muslin cords of her nightcap. "I'm going to count to ten. Then I'll light a lamp and greet our visitors." She raised her eyes heavenward. "Lord, protect us . . . and forgive me for my deception."

My mother never ceases to amaze me. It took less than five minutes of feminine outrage before the men fled Locust Hill in a flurry of apologies for disturbing our rest.

Jess flips through the remaining pages of the journal. "It looks like that's the last entry."

"What?!" Kelly nearly jumps out of her chair. "That's all Anna wrote?"

"Apparently so," says Jess, again paging through the rest of the journal.

Marina whistles. "Nothing like leaving a person on the edge of her seat. There's gotta be more."

"Wait a minute." Jess pulls a thin, folded sheet from between the yellowed pages. "This looks like it might be an old letter."

"Really?" asks Lucy. "Who is it from?"

With a frown of concentration on her face, Jess carefully unfolds the brittle page. "Let's see . . ."

■ ■ ■ ■

CHAPTER
TWENTY-THREE

■ ■ ■ ■

Sour Cherry Pie

Crust:
2 1/4 cups flour
1/2 teaspoon salt
5 oz. vegetable shortening
1/3 cup ice water

Cherry Filling:
2/3 cup sugar
1/2 teaspoon cinnamon
4 tablespoons cornstarch
1 1/2 cups cherry juice
3 lb. frozen cherries (with sugar)
1 1/2 tablespoons vegetable shortening
1 tablespoon vanilla
1/2 tablespoon milk
2 teaspoons sugar

Instructions

1. For crust, combine flour and salt in

food processor.

2. Add shortening to food processor. Pulse until mixture looks like small peas.

3. Add ice water and pulse until dough begins to stick together. Remove and form dough into two balls. Cover and refrigerate for 30 minutes.

4. For filling, combine sugar, cinnamon, and cornstarch in saucepan. Add cherry juice and cook until mixture is thick and bubbly.

5. Stir and boil for one minute. Add cherries and cook until it starts to boil again.

6. Remove from heat and add shortening and vanilla extract.

7. Remove refrigerated dough.

8. On lightly floured surface, roll bottom crust into circle one inch larger than pie plate.

9. Gently ease dough into pie plate. Trim edge even with pie plate.

10. Spoon cherry filling into prepared pastry.

11. Roll out top crust the same way and gently place over filling. Brush top crust with milk and sprinkle with sugar.

12. Bake at 350 degrees for 40–45 minutes or until crust is golden brown.

Benton Barracks, near St. Louis, Missouri
May 10, 1863
My dearest Emily,

It has been a long time since I have had a spare minute to write, so great are the needs of my present assignment. However, I gladly seize this opportunity to scrawl a few lines and let you know that I am among the living.

The longer I am stationed at this post, the more I realize that the hospital here is exceptional. This is extremely advantageous since Missouri, as a border state, is near the site of many battles with high numbers of wounded. The state also has many Confederate sympathizers, and it is especially heartbreaking to hear tales of brother fighting against brother.

The hospital is enclosed, thoroughly ventilated, and furnished with good beds. Now that it is complete, it is capable of accommodating 2,500 patients. And trust me, my dear, all of those beds are needed to care for the wounded.

As is expected from such a fine facility, the patient mortality rate is quite low. While this news is heartening, it pains me to see the care of the colored troops who have journeyed north to assist the Union Army.

In the Second Missouri Colored Infantry,

I am sad to report that more than a hundred men died before the regiment even took the field. These brave men, having enlisted of their own volition throughout the state, after making a long, perilous journey north, were forwarded to this post during the winter season. They were not only starving, but thinly clad, hatless, and shoeless. Many of these men had already undergone amputation of their frozen feet or hands — with many dying as a result of infection. It is disheartening to see the indifference many of the troops demonstrate for the colored regiments. Thus, I am sad to report, the level of care offered to the colored troops is substandard — especially when compared to that given to the white regiments.

On that subject, I have some unfortunate news to report. Big Henry has contracted smallpox. As is the regulation, he must be relocated to the smallpox hospital located on an island in the Mississippi River. Henry has been such a true and loyal friend both in the field and at this post that I could not, in good conscience, trust his care to an unknown practitioner. Thus, I requested a transfer to work at the island hospital.

Do not worry for my safety, my dear, for the island is one place the rebel forces do not dare tread for fear of contracting the disease. As I told Henry when he attempted to dissuade me from accompanying him, I'd rather dodge pox than bullets.

Since my relocation to the island, I do not have easy access to the mail, so my letters may be few. But please know that I would give anything in the world to see you and Anna and enjoy a large slice of your delicious sour cherry pie on our own front porch. Unfortunately, I have no idea when I might have that pleasure. I had hoped it would have been by Christmas, but now we both know that was not to be.

I must close for fear I do not get to send my letter off. My love and a thousand kisses to my own sweet Emily and dear Anna. Good-bye, for the present. I think of you and pray for you every day we are apart. I dream of the day we can be together again.

As ever,
Your loving husband,
J. C. Simmons

"That's it," Jess proclaims, folding the letter and slipping it back in the journal. "No other entries or letters."

Marina is already on her feet. "Are you *sure* there're no more entries, Jess? I can't believe Anna would leave us hanging like this."

"Marina, this is a young girl's journal, not a drugstore novel."

"I'm sorry, but I *have* to know the end of this story. I wanna know what happened to Joseph and Big Henry. Did they come back from the war? And Anna and Emily . . . what happened with them? I'm serious; I won't be able to sleep until I find out."

"Lucy, do you think your Aunt Bette might know the rest of the story?" asks Mary Alice.

"I don't know. Maybe."

"Let's ask her," Kelly insists. "Janelle told me she plans to give Aunt Bette a ride to church in the morning. Why don't we invite them both to dinner afterward?"

"We can certainly ask them," says Lucy. "I'd also like a chance to apologize for my harsh words last night."

"Hold on," I interrupt. "I'd like to set up this little soiree, too, but I want to know who you think will be cooking this dinner? I'll make breakfast, and then I go off duty."

"Whoa, Lizzie!" Marina exclaims. "Don't get your undies in a bundle, girlfriend."

"Very funny. But I'm serious."

"We'll take them to Sally's," says Kelly.

"I've been craving that coconut pie for weeks."

Marina gives a thumbs-up. "Sounds like a plan. But I still don't know how I'm going to get to sleep tonight without knowing what happened to Joseph and Big Henry . . . or Anna and Emily and that young family on the run. It's like going to bed in the middle of *CSI*."

"Don't worry, Rina, we have lots of yard work to do," Jess suggests. "I'll tire you out."

"Me and my big mouth."

■ ■ ■ ■

CHAPTER
TWENTY-FOUR

■ ■ ■ ■

BAKED EGGS WITH SMOKED SALMON AND CREAM CHEESE

10 eggs
1/2 cup milk
3 oz. cream cheese with chives
8 oz. smoked salmon
1/4 cup butter
1 tablespoon chopped fresh dill (or 1 teaspoon dried)
1 cup prepared hollandaise sauce (optional)

Instructions

1. Beat eggs and milk together in a large bowl. Fold in cream cheese, and smoked salmon.
2. Melt butter in a 7×12-inch casserole dish. Pour egg mixture into the pan.
3. Sprinkle dill over top. Bake at 350 degrees for 30 minutes until set.

4. Serve hot with hollandaise sauce, if desired.

Autumn Fruit Salad

2 red apples
2 green apples
2 pears
2 sliced bananas
8 oz. seedless red grapes
8 oz. seedless green grapes
1/2 cup sliced natural almonds, toasted
1 cup vanilla yogurt
1 teaspoon cinnamon
1/4 teaspoon ground ginger
1/2 teaspoon nutmeg
2 tablespoons apple juice or cider

Instructions

1. Wash, core, and slice apples and pears. Slice bananas 1/2-inch thick. Wash grapes and cut in half.
2. Combine fruit and almonds in a bowl.
3. Mix remaining ingredients.
4. Pour over fruit salad and stir to coat fruit evenly.
5. Chill before serving.

There's something inherently peaceful about waking up in the country. Instead of being startled by an alarm clock, lawn mower, or city traffic, I awaken gently as the rising sun quietly shoos away the night. Taking a long, catlike stretch in my sun-filled bedroom at Locust Hill, I think this must be how God intended the rest cycle — before the age of artificial illumination tangled up our biorhythms.

I sigh in satisfaction, noting that the spot in the bed next to me is empty. That means Marina has taken off on her predawn run without rousing me. Standing up to my bossy friends might just become a habit.

While brushing my teeth at the bathroom sink, I notice that I have a serious case of bed head. I'll have to wash my hair. Knowing from experience that anything having to do with my hair is a lengthy process, I decide to get breakfast going before my shower.

I pad down the stairs to the kitchen in my bare feet, wishing I would have taken a few minutes to dig out my slippers from my overnight bag. After lighting the old oven, per Janelle's instructions, I set a pot of coffee up to brew. Uttering a quick prayer of gratitude that the house didn't blow up, I put the casserole — Baked Eggs with

Smoked Salmon and Cream Cheese — I had assembled the prior evening in the oven and head upstairs to shower before church.

At the top of the stairs, I see that one of my friends has had the same idea. Heading back to the kitchen — once again chastising myself for forgetting to grab my slippers — I decide to put together my Autumn Fruit Salad.

I mix up a dressing of vanilla yogurt, spices, and apple cider before noticing that the water has shut off upstairs. Once again I head up to the bathroom, thinking Marina's workout will have nothing on me after climbing all these stairs. Just as I round the corner, I see the bathroom door closing.

Letting out a sigh of frustration, I decide to pass the time by finishing my salad. After slicing fresh apples, pears, and grapes and tossing them with the dressing, I cock my head to see if I can hear water running upstairs. Hearing none, I decide to make another go at a turn in the bathroom. Before I reach the stairs, Marina bounds in the front door.

"Hey, Liz! What are you doing up so early?"

"I was just putting breakfast on, and now I thought I'd —"

"So that's what that great smell is! I can't

wait to dig in as soon as I grab a shower." She charges up the stairs.

Remember, Liz, patience is a virtue, I tell myself, taking a cleansing breath to reinforce the concept. Checking on my casserole, I decide to grab a cup of coffee and take advantage of a little quiet time.

In the freshly wallpapered library, I settle into a wing chair with a copy of the *Daily Light.* As always, the truth of God's Word calms my spirit. I am so immersed that I hate to respond to the minute timer that indicates my casserole is done.

On the way to the kitchen, I see Jess and Lucy coming down the stairs.

"Good morning, ladies," I say in a much better mood.

Jess yawns. "Hi, Liz. I didn't know you were up."

"Jess, how could you not know . . . with that heavenly smell coming from the kitchen," says Lucy.

I smile in response to her compliment.

"So what is that wonderful smell, Lizzie?" asks Jess.

"Secret recipe," I tease. "Hey, is the bathroom open?"

"I think so," Lucy replies. "I saw Marina in the hall."

"Great! Jess, would you check on the casserole? It's probably done . . . and there's a fruit salad in the fridge."

"Sure, but —"

"I'm going to try to sneak in the shower."

Once again my plans are thwarted by the sound of running water behind the closed bathroom door. I slide down the wall, resigned to the fact that the only way I'll get a turn is by standing vigil outside the door. Some things never change.

■ ■ ■ ■

CHAPTER
TWENTY-FIVE

■ ■ ■ ■

TCC Cinnamon Rolls

1 (3 lb.) package frozen bread dough,
  thawed in package
1 cup butter, melted
1 cup brown sugar
1 tablespoon cinnamon
1 cup heavy cream
Vanilla or cream cheese frosting

Instructions

1. Punch down thawed dough and let
   rest 5 minutes. Roll out on floured
   surface into a 15×24-inch rectangle.
2. For filling, brush dough liberally
   with melted butter. Mix brown
   sugar and cinnamon; sprinkle over
   buttered dough.
3. Roll up dough, jelly-roll fashion.
   Cut into 24 slices.
4. Place cinnamon roll slices in two,

well greased 9×13-inch pans. Let rise in warm place until dough is doubled in bulk, about 45 minutes.
5. Pour cream over top of rolls.
6. Preheat oven to 350 degrees. Bake 20–25 minutes, or until rolls are nicely browned.
7. Cool rolls slightly and spread with frosting.

MELT-IN-YOUR-MOUTH POT ROAST

3 lb. beef roast (any kind, except brisket)
1 can cream of mushroom soup
1 envelope dry onion soup mix
1 (16 oz.) package baby carrots

Instructions

1. Put roast in Crock-Pot.
2. Top with onion soup and mushroom soup. Add carrots.
3. Cook covered on low 8–10 hours, or high 5–6 hours.

MOM'S BANANA PUDDING

1 1/4 cups sugar, plus 3/4 cup
4 tablespoons flour
4 cups milk
6 eggs, separated
2 teaspoons vanilla

4 tablespoons butter
1 box vanilla wafers
5–6 ripe bananas

Instructions

1. Mix sugar, flour, milk, and egg yolks.
2. Cook on low heat, stirring constantly, until thick. Remove from heat and stir in vanilla and butter until butter is melted.
3. Arrange 3/4 of the box of vanilla wafers on the bottom of 2 1/2-quart baking dish. Pour 1/3 of pudding over wafers. Layer sliced bananas on pudding. Pour remaining pudding on bananas.
4. Beat egg whites until stiff, add 3/4 cup sugar, and continue beating until stiff. Spread over pudding.
5. Bake at 350 degrees until meringue is lightly browned, about 10–12 minutes.

The morning service at Tredway Community Church was as diverse as its members. Young and old, black and white came together to worship God in a variety of music styles — from rousing spirituals to traditional hymns. And judging from the sheer volume of the clapping, singing, and shouting, our praise was easily heard in heaven!

Normally, such a nontraditional service and diverse congregation in small-town Nebraska would have taken me by surprise. But after getting a glimpse of the commitment and bravery of the town's founders through Anna's journal, I began to understand that among brothers and sisters in Christ, colors fade and walls tumble. I hated to see the service come to a close.

As I chat with Janelle now, after the service, I learn that the church has a small but apparently very committed congregation. Only one of their fifty members is absent from morning services — and only because a horse has begun to foal this morning, she tells me.

"Do you always have such good attendance?" I ask as we munch on homemade cinnamon rolls in the narthex.

"Usually, 'cept the time a nest of spiders took over the choir loft."

"Spiders?" I ask, looking around nervously.

"Yep. I never saw Darlene jump so high . . . and I don't expect to see it again."

"So, I assume you were able to take care of the problem?"

"Sure," replies Janelle with a wink. "At least that's what we told Darlene."

If there was ever a reason to make a graceful exit, this is it. I hate spiders. I tell Janelle we'll see her and Aunt Bette at the diner, grab Marina's arm, and head for the car.

I'm disappointed there is no blue plate special at Sally's on Sunday. But from the large number of customers crowding the little diner, it doesn't appear to be hurting business.

"That's only for the weekdays — and Saturday, of course," explains the proprietor, who we find out also pitches in to wait tables on the weekend. "But I make pot roast on Sundays. It's guaranteed to melt in your mouth."

If the savory smell emanating from the kitchen is any indication, I can't wait to test her claim. Marina, Jess, and I peruse the menu at a large table while we wait for the rest of our group to arrive with Aunt Bette and Janelle. Once again I'm grateful for

Mary Alice's foresight in calling to make a reservation — a first for Sally.

"Melt-in-your-mouth pot roast sounds good enough to me," Marina proclaims. "I'll take it . . . with all the fixin's you can fit on the plate, whatever color it is."

"I've always admired a woman with a healthy appetite." The familiar voice across the room turns out to be Jeff, peeking around the back booth in which he's seated.

"When did you sneak in?" asks Marina in a voice that causes a hush to fall over the restaurant.

I'm on the edge of my seat, unable to keep visions of *Gunfight at the OK Corral* from my mind.

"Last time I looked, it was still a free country, Lieutenant," replies Jeff, rising from his booth and strolling to the table. "I wouldn't miss Sally's Melt-in-Your-Mouth Pot Roast for the world."

"Jeff, would you like to join us?" asks Jess. "That is, if you can forgive my friend's rude behavior."

"Hey!" Marina demands. "What did I do that was rude?"

"Don't worry, Jessie." Jeff smiles. "I can hold my own with Marina."

"Sounds like a challenge to me," Marina fires back.

"Play nice, children." Sally winks at Jeff as she heads to the kitchen to get our iced tea.

Sally's pot roast truly did melt in my mouth. In fact, I would rate this dinner as one of the top culinary experiences of my adult life. (After all, nothing will ever compare to my mom's banana pudding.) I thought about tipping off the restaurant critic at the paper to Sally's Diner but thought better of it. Sally didn't seem to need the business. And it might just annoy all the locals in Tredway if a bunch of "outsiders" poured into town and disrupted their peaceful, well-ordered week.

With nine in our party, we are now polishing off an entire coconut cream pie for dessert. I justify the nagging guilt for my gluttony by recounting all the hard work I have done this weekend. I employed the same strategy yesterday after eating Janelle's Banana Split Cake — and all those brownies the night before. It worked then, and I have no reason to doubt its effectiveness now.

As we enjoy our dessert, I can tell my friends are as anxious as I am to find out what else Aunt Bette knows about the Simmons family. We had all reluctantly promised Lucy that we would let her bring up the subject. As it turned out, it was unnecessary.

"Well, ladies, I must say, I am very impressed with your restraint," says Aunt Bette, delicately dabbing her lips with a napkin. "Lucy told me after church that you finished my grandmother's journal yesterday afternoon. I'm surprised I didn't see you last night, demanding to hear the end of the story."

"See, Luce?" Marina raises her dark eyebrows. "I told you we shoulda gone over to Orrick."

"I guess I still feel a little sheepish about my behavior," says Lucy with a catch in her voice. "All those terrible things I said about our family when we uncovered the secret room. Can you ever forgive me, Aunt Bette?" Lucy stares down at her hands.

"Oh, my dear, of course I forgive you." The old woman reaches across the table to take Lucy's hand. "Just as I hope you'll forgive me for all the intrigue. I felt it was important for you to uncover our family history yourself."

"I hope you'll forgive my part too," says Janelle. "I sure felt sneaky leavin' that letter in the front hall and not sayin' a word about it. I sure hope you don't hold that against me."

Lucy looks up, surprise on her face. "Of course, I forgive you . . . both of you. But I'm still not sure why you felt it was so important for me to find the letter myself."

Aunt Bette smiles gently. "It's taken me a long time to understand that we often learn less from what people tell us than by discovering truth and history for ourselves." She stops to pat her white hair, which is smoothed into a chignon at the nape of her neck. "Now, don't I sound all philosophical, Janelle?"

Janelle laughs. "Sure do. Mama would be proud."

Aunt Bette returns a knowing smile.

"Seriously, that makes a lot of sense, Aunt Bette," Lucy says. "In fact, I've often told Alli that I learn the most from the *process* of struggling through an issue."

"Well, I'll tell you what *I* learned through the process this weekend," Marina claims, pointing at Jessie. "Behind that sweet exterior is a cruel taskmaster. It was so dark before we came in last night that I couldn't even see the plants I was putting in."

"Sissy," Jess teases.

"How can you say that? Look at my manicure!" Marina woefully examines her once perfect but now chipped nails.

Jeff snorts. "Now I have heard everything."

Marina gives him a playful punch on the shoulder.

"Count your blessings, Jess," Kelly adds. "I had to work with the queen of the chalk line."

"Don't even think about going there, Kel," I warn.

"I'm just kidding, Liz. I know I gave you a hard time. Forgive me?" asks Kelly with pleading, puppy-dog eyes.

I sigh dramatically. "I already have. I'm *that* kind of person."

A corporate groan.

"Actually, Liz, you really came through in the kitchen," says Jess. "I have to get the recipe for that casserole you made for breakfast this morning."

"On one condition," I reply. "If Janelle gives me the recipe for her Banana Split Cake. I am still dreaming about the luscious pairing of strawberries, pineapple, and hot fudge."

Janelle lets out a hearty laugh. "Lizzie, you are my kind of gal!"

"I'm not usually the one getting us back on track," Mary Alice interrupts politely, "but I am *dying* to know what happened to the Simmons family."

"Well, Janelle," says Aunt Bette, "would you like to start or shall I?"

"You go on ahead, Miss Henrietta. I'll fill in as need be."

"Very well, dear," replies Aunt Bette. "Just like all of you, I had a head full of questions after I finished reading my grandmother's journal. And, unfortunately, those most likely to have known the answers had already passed on."

Marina raises her hand. "Sorry to interrupt, but I need to keep things straight in my mind. Anna Simmons was your grandmother, right?"

"That's right, dear. Her married name was Crawford."

"Like yours," says Mary Alice. "So her son must have been your father?"

Aunt Bette smiles at Mary Alice across the table. "Exactly. You have a talent for genealogy, my dear."

Mary Alice smiles shyly.

"As I said, by the time I found my grandmother's journal, all I had left in the way of family history were some scraps of conversation I remembered having with my grandmother when I was a little girl and, of course, what was recorded in the family Bible."

"You still have the old Simmons Bible?" I blurt out. *This is getting interesting.*

"Yes, dear, I do. My grandmother, Anna,

passed it to my mother . . . and she to me. I always intended for it to go to your mother, Lucy, when I passed on."

This time Lucy is the one to reach for Aunt Bette's hand as tears threaten to spill from her lashes.

"I do miss your mother, dear. She was very special to me."

"I miss her too."

"I didn't mean to get all maudlin." Aunt Bette takes out a lace-trimmed handkerchief and quietly blows her nose. "Let me tell you what I was able to piece together. Unfortunately, her father and my great-grandfather, Joseph Simmons, never returned from the war. It appears he died of smallpox while stationed in Missouri."

"Was that recorded in the family Bible?" asks Lucy.

"Just basic information — the date, location, and cause of his death. He is buried at Jefferson Barracks Cemetery near St. Louis."

"That's so sad," says Mary Alice. "I guess Big Henry must have died too."

"That's what I assumed until I did a little more digging. Lois, down at the hall of records, helped me sort through a bunch of old documents."

I am always amazed at how much history

is tucked inside seemingly boring public documents. For a nosy reporter like me, pulling open a dusty, old file cabinet is like opening a sunken treasure chest. "So what'd you find?" I ask.

Aunt Bette raises her eyebrows conspiratorially. "The most useful piece of information was Joseph's will. By the date, it appears he wrote it just before he was transferred to the island to care for smallpox patients. This is what he alluded to in his letter. I'm assuming you read it?"

"As you said earlier, Aunt Bette," Kelly says, laughing, "we may be old, but we are not dead."

"Well put, my dear." Aunt Bette chuckles. "Well, Joseph's will was a little unusual because he included his reasons behind the disposition of his property and assets."

"So he emphasized the testament part of his last will and testament," says Mary Alice.

"That's exactly right, my dear," replies Aunt Bette. "I suspect he didn't want to worry his family, but as a doctor, he knew very well the risk he was taking by moving to the island. Joseph must have believed it was important for his wife and daughter to know why he felt compelled to request the transfer."

"Aunt Bette, you're killing me here," complains Marina. "I can't stand the suspense. What'd the will say?"

"She *is* very direct, isn't she, dear?" asks Aunt Bette, tilting her head toward Marina but looking at me.

I laugh. "*Direct* is putting it mildly."

"I guess I do have trouble getting to — how do you young people put it? — getting to the *chase.*"

Marina sighs.

I flash her a stern look.

She shrugs and looks away.

"Very well, I won't torture you any longer, dear," says Aunt Bette with a wink. "In his will, Joseph relayed an incident in which his base had been attacked by Confederate sympathizers in the middle of the night. Big Henry, who was housed in a nearby barracks, had put his own life in peril to alert Joseph and lead him to safety. Joseph credited Henry with saving his life."

"That's so cool," I say. "Joseph helped Henry when he needed a safe place, and Henry was able to return the favor."

"Greater love has no one than this, that one lay down his life for his friends," whispers Lucy.

"John 15:13," adds Jess.

For a quiet moment, no one speaks.

"Joseph also noted that he hoped God would give him the chance to share these experiences with his family in person," Aunt Bette continues. "But if that were not to be the case, he felt there should be a record to help them understand his last wishes. The will specified that if Henry survived him, Joseph's gold watch and medical instruments should be sold . . . with the money given to Henry to finance his move west.

"So he could follow his dream," I surmise.

"That's not all," adds Aunt Bette. "The will also contained Joseph's wishes that a quarter section of his land, as well as the old cabin, be made available to Henry to farm as long as he desired."

"That's very generous," says Kelly, "but I thought Big Henry wanted to run cattle out West."

"I've always suspected Joseph included this stipulation in the will to help Henry raise the necessary funds to purchase and stock a cattle ranch."

"That would allow him to be his own boss," I reason.

"For the first time in his life," Lucy says in a low tone, "Henry would be his own master."

Silence reigns for a moment before Marina pipes up. "So did Big Henry survive the war? Did he ever come back to Tred-way?"

"Janelle, why don't you take the story from here?" Aunt Bette pats her longtime friend on the hand.

We all look at Janelle quizzically.

What does she have to do with this story? I think.

Before she utters a word, her wide smile answers my question.

"You are a descendant of Big Henry," I say.

Janelle smiles even wider. "Henry Miller was my great-great-granddaddy."

"No!" Jess exclaims.

Then, as if on cue, our questions spill out at once.

"So he survived the smallpox epidemic?" asks Mary Alice.

"Are you saying Big Henry settled in Tred-way?" asks Marina.

"Why didn't Henry move west as he'd always dreamed?" asks Kelly.

Janelle answers with her warm laugh. "Slow down, ladies! One at a time! I'm an old woman!"

"Not that old!" exclaims Aunt Bette.

More laughter. When we finally settle down, Janelle continues. "Here is where things get a little foggy. After Miss Henrietta found her grandmama's journal, we began to piece together what we knew from both families."

"I must admit," giggles Aunt Bette, "I felt a bit like Inspector Holmes."

Janelle grins. "So I guess that makes me —"

"My dear Watson!" exclaims Aunt Bette.

Both women break out in laughter at their own joke.

While the rest of us chuckle politely, Marina points to her watch.

Still giggling, Aunt Bette says, "We better get back to the story, dear. I think our hostesses are losing patience."

Janelle sputters and takes a drink of water. "All right then, I'll go on with my story. I remember my granny tellin' me she was born in the old cabin behind Locust Hill. She lived there as a little girl with her parents and grandparents. Her name was Mary Miller. Her granddaddy was Henry."

Aunt Bette leans forward. "And I remembered that my grandmother always spoke fondly of a man named Henry who used to live in the old cabin."

"I think I saw it when we were working in the garden," says Jess. "Just west of the orchard, right?"

Aunt Bette nods. "That's it."

"Is this the cabin the Simmons lived in while Joseph finished the house?" I ask.

"I would think so," replies Aunt Bette. "Until I found my grandmother's diary, I assumed Henry must have been a hired hand."

"I wonder if he came back after the war to look after Emily and Anna," I muse.

"That's my guess, dear," Aunt Bette adds. "I remember my grandmother saying, 'Henry took good care of us.'"

"But Henry had been through so much already," says Lucy. "Surely he deserved to . . ."

"Yes, he did," says Aunt Bette, answering Lucy's unspoken question. "But some people make a different choice for the sake of someone they love."

Again, silence reigns. I look around the table at the faces of my friends and realize we're all probably thinking the same thing. We had expected our FAC at Locust Hill to be a girlfriends' getaway, with a little work on the side. What we hadn't planned on was the work taking place in our hearts. All because of events that took place a long time ago.

Marina, the detective, doesn't miss a beat. "OK. So, we have a pretty good idea of what happened to Joseph and Big Henry. But you still haven't spilled the beans on Anna and Emily. Why didn't Anna finish her story?"

"Marina, this is not a novel!" I exclaim. "It's real life. Real people. Stuff happens."

"Ouch!" says Marina. "I just asked a simple question."

Jess covers my hand with hers, signaling me not to take Marina's bait. "Maybe Anna quit writing in her journal when she found out about her father's death," she suggests. "It might have been too painful."

"Also, she and her mother were left alone in Nebraska, which was definitely in the middle of nowhere back then," Lucy adds. "They had enough to do just to survive. It had to be frightening for them."

Marina shakes her head. "From the way Anna described her mom, I wouldn't call Emily Simmons a shrinking violet."

"Definitely not," says Aunt Bette. "Despite her youthful naiveté and early fears about working with the Underground Railroad, neither was my grandmother. After the war both Emily and Anna became very active in the women's groups that formed to support missionary work here and abroad. In fact, before she married, Anna served as a missionary for ten years among displaced African Americans in Mississippi."

"What about Emily?" asks Lucy. "I find it

hard to believe Anna would leave her mother all alone."

"I wouldn't be surprised if it was Emily's idea," replies Aunt Bette. "You'd do the same thing, dear. I can't imagine you'd want to keep your daughter from answering God's call on her life."

"Of course not, but things are different now."

"The years may pass, but people are still the same. There are many ways a mother can keep her children tied to her — both spoken and unspoken. And sometimes with the best of intentions."

Once again, I try to put myself in Emily's place. What if Katie wanted to go to the mission field? And what if she felt called to the Middle East, where in some countries people — including women — are beheaded simply for speaking out about their faith? Would I try to talk her out of it?

Maybe.

Probably.

Definitely.

And what would be my reasoning? Am I more concerned about my child's safety? Or am I more afraid about how *I* would survive if something should happen to my child?

I hate self-examination.

I shiver in spite of the warmth of Sally's Diner. Luckily I don't have to venture too far into the depths of my psyche. I can always count on Marina to change the subject.

"So any more information you two are still keeping close to the vest?"

Even Aunt Bette's wrinkles smile at this question. "No, that's about all I know. What do you think, Janelle? Have we forgotten anything?"

"No, other than what's up on the hill. They might wanna see the inscriptions."

"You're absolutely right," declares Aunt Bette. "There's a tombstone in the cemetery near the church that marks Big Henry's grave. I think you might find the inscription interesting."

"Perhaps we can stop by on our way out of town," Lucy suggests.

"If you do, you might also want to read the stones marking Emily's and Anna's graves. It's amazing what you can find out in a graveyard."

"Graveyard!" Marina shivers. "That reminds me. How did the rumor about Locust Hill's being some sort of haunted house get started?"

There's a twinkle in Aunt Bette's blue eyes. "Think about it, my dear. If you were women living alone, conducting secret activities, would you consider dispelling such a convenient rumor?"

Marina whistles. "Very crafty."

"Well now, ladies," Aunt Bette announces, pushing back her chair, "I will ask if one of you is willing to bring me home to Orrick. I am overdue for my afternoon nap."

"Oh yes," agrees Janelle. "How I look forward to the sweet Sabbath!"

Since by now it's already late Sunday afternoon and our families will be wondering where we are, Kelly and Mary Alice agree to drop Janelle at the church to collect her car and then close up Locust Hill. The rest of us drive Aunt Bette home. On the way back, Lucy asks if Marina minds stopping by the Tredway cemetery.

It doesn't take long to find Emily's simple grave marker. It lists her name, dates of birth and death, and a Scripture reference.

I stop to do a little math. "Wait a minute. This says Emily died in 1873. If Anna was in the mission field for ten years . . ."

"Her mother had to have died before she returned from Mississippi," says Lucy, a tremor in her voice. "I wonder if she ever saw her again?"

As Lucy jots down the Scripture reference

from the gravestone — Micah 6:8 — Marina calls to us from an adjacent section of the cemetery: "I think I found Big Henry's grave."

After reading the inscription on Henry's marker, we drive back to Omaha. I'm not surprised that our conversation is subdued. While I think about Joseph, Emily, Anna — even Aunt Bette — my thoughts keep going back to Big Henry. In spite of all the hardship and indignity he weathered throughout his life, the inscription on his gravestone remains an enduring, powerful testament to his deep faith and strong character.

IF EVER THE SUN SHONE IN THE HEART OF A MAN, IT SHONE IN THE HEART OF HENRY MILLER.

■ ■ ■ ■

CHAPTER
TWENTY-SIX

■ ■ ■ ■

Cowpoke Chicken

6 boneless, skinless chicken breasts
2/3 cup cream cheese with chives
6 slices bacon
1/2 cup ranch dressing
1/2 cup salsa

Instructions

1. Put a dollop of cream cheese in the center of each chicken breast.
2. Roll the breast up and wrap with a slice of bacon.
3. Bake at 350 degrees for 25 minutes, or until chicken is no longer pink in the center.
4. Meanwhile, mix dressing and salsa. Serve with chicken.

Tropical Pie

1 (16 oz.) can crushed pineapple, undrained
1 (3 oz.) box vanilla instant pudding
1 cup sour cream
1 vanilla cookie crust (or graham cracker crust)
3 cups nondairy topping (Cool Whip) or whipped cream
1/4 cup toasted coconut, if desired

Instructions

1. Mix pineapple, pudding, and sour cream. Put into crust.
2. Chill for 2 hours.
3. Top with whipped topping and coconut (if desired) before serving.

Audrey's Strawberry Spinach Salad

1 bag fresh spinach
16 oz. fresh strawberries, sliced
1 cup mozzarella cheese, shredded
1/2 red onion, thinly sliced
1/2 cup pecans
2 tablespoons lime juice
2 tablespoons sugar
1/4 cup vegetable oil
2 tablespoons vinegar

Instructions

1. Toss spinach, strawberries, cheese, onions, and pecans in a large salad bowl.
2. For dressing, whisk together lime juice, sugar, oil, and vinegar.
3. Just before serving, pour over spinach mixture.

After the FAC weekend in Tredway, I float into my home in Omaha, buoyed by the human spirit. A spirit that would risk all to fight injustice, to minister to a friend, to train up a child. My own spirit soars as I contemplate the various causes I might champion to better the world for future generations.

It's probably good that I'm soaring, because as soon as I step into the kitchen, reality hits. I feel the familiar *riiippppp* of my foot sticking to the kitchen floor.

This cannot be the same floor I mopped on Thursday, can it? Could I be at the wrong address? What happened to the house I worked so hard to put in order before I left?

Before I can fully ponder these questions, Daisy comes charging around the corner, with my son in hot pursuit.

"Hi, Mom," Josh calls. "What's for dinner?"

I carefully rein in the hateful hag's leash before she can answer in my stead. "I missed you, too, sweetheart," I reply carefully.

"Mom, we need to talk. Dad made *hamburgers* for dinner last night."

"Great. I know you like —"

"Mom, you're not getting it. That's *all* he made. Hamburgers."

"I thought you liked — ," I try again.

"You're not listening, Mom. The whole dinner was a hamburger on a bun. Not even a bag of chips. I'm thinking I oughta take an extra vitamin or something."

Before I can respond, I hear the voice of my elder daughter, Katie.

"Is that Mom?" she shouts from the second floor in an earsplitting outdoor voice.

I cover my ears. "I just got home, Kate. Come on down. I want to give you a hug."

When she obliges quickly, I know something's up. After a two-second embrace, Katie fills me in on the real reason for her concern.

"Mom, you have to talk to Dad. He bought this dog food at the grocery store from some guy pretending to be a vet. Dad said it was cheaper than the stuff you usually buy for Daisy, and it's supposed to leave 'less residue,' whatever that means."

"If it's made by a vet, I'm sure —"

"Mom, it looks like little worms, and it made Daisy sick. She threw up all over the family room again. It was disgusting, and Dad made me clean it up. I know he just bought that dog food because it was cheap."

"Katie, you should be happy your dad is frugal because —"

"Hi, Mommy!" shouts Hannah, popping up like a jack-in-the-box from behind the sofa.

I guess there's no hope of finishing a conversation tonight. So I simply open my arms for a hug. "Hi, sweetheart, did you miss me?"

"Um, yes, but . . ." Hannah takes a deep breath, as if deciding whether to continue.

"What's wrong, sweetie?"

Another long breath. This time a little shaky.

"I'm quitting my volleyball team."

I'm puzzled. "But, Hannah, you love volleyball. Why would —"

"I can't go back! It's too embarrassing!"

"What happened, honey?"

"It was my turn for treats and . . ."

"I know. Your dad said he would pick up the treats before the game. Did he forget?"

"I wish."

"Hannah, what — ," I attempt.

"Mommy, he got the most embarrassing treats! He bought those little drink boxes that have a picture of Winnie the Pooh on them. And each girl didn't even get her own brownie."

"I heard that," says my husband, who's just coming in from the garage. "I've already told you, Hannah, the box said it contained ten brownies. How would I know they put two in a package?"

Hannah rolls her eyes in response.

"We obviously missed you, Liz." John gives me a long hug.

"I missed all of you too. A lot." And I surprise myself — I really mean it.

"About that new dog food." John hesitates. "I guess it didn't agree with Daisy. I've looked all over for the carpet cleaner, but . . ." He shrugs in a silent apology.

As I head to the laundry room to retrieve the carpet cleaner, I smile. While I may not be a June Cleaver–type mom, my family actually missed my mothering. While being proficient in the areas of volleyball treats, meal planning, and canine care may not be valued in all circles, these skills are valued in the circle I care about most. *My* family circle. And that feels good.

Maybe it's the country air . . . or maybe I'm losing my mind, but I have a little spring in my step as I toss the carpet cleaner to John and head upstairs to unpack.

Loving Life!
By Elizabeth Harris
    You may have noticed, faithful readers, that my column has a new title. The purpose

of this bold move is to reflect a new, and hopefully exciting, direction. Instead of "The Lovely Life," my prose will hence be known as "Loving Life!"

I beg your indulgence as I explain my thinking behind this title. According to the dictionary, the adjective *lovely* is used to describe a person or object that **appears** attractive to others, whereas the verb *loving* means "to cherish or hold dear." Faithful readers, I have come to realize that it is ultimately unfulfilling to pursue a life that merely appears attractive to the outside world. In this quest for external perfection, we often miss the inherent beauty of the life with which we have been blessed. I encourage you, precious reader, to join me in LOVING LIFE — by embracing your unique personality and present situation.

Not one to offer advice without testing the "proverbial" waters, I recently applied this philosophy to my present situation. Recently it was my turn to host a dinner party, and I found myself with little time for either planning or preparation. I called on my favorite entertaining guru, Lynnette from Campbell Creative Catering, and confessed my dilemma. Without batting an eye, Lynnette suggested I host a "tacky" dinner party.

Although tempted to end the conversation, fearing Lynnette had suffered her own "lovely life" meltdown, I asked her to explain the concept further. Her ideas are outlined below:

1. Send simple invitations, instructing guests to wear their "tackiest" party clothes and bring a "tacky" gift to exchange with other guests.
2. Table settings and decorations may be as tacky as you like. Lynnette sug-

gested using up leftover paper products from past celebrations.

3. Circulate tacky hors d'oeuvres to guests as they arrive.

4. After all guests are present, divide them into four teams. Inform each team that members are responsible for shopping, preparing, and serving a portion of the evening's dinner. Give each team a bag of coins to pay for their assigned course: salad, entrée, side dishes, or dessert.

5. Relax while guests are busy shopping and preparing dinner.

6. After dinner, supervise the tacky-gift exchange.

Although a bit apprehensive — but even more desperate — I decided to go with Lynnette's tacky theme. I set the table with an eclectic mix of birthday, baby shower, and graduation tableware. For hors d'oeuvres I served slices of ring bologna atop saltine crackers to guests in fabulously tacky attire. The plaid leisure suit and prom dress teamed with a pair of hiking boots were my personal favorites.

I was relieved to see how my guests eagerly rose to our tacky challenge by preparing a delicious meal. We enjoyed tender Cowpoke Chicken, rice casserole, and Audrey's Strawberry Spinach Salad — topped off by a creamy Tropical Pie — all simple recipes I will add to my personal file.

The gift exchange was a big hit. My husband received a secondhand electric nose-hair trimmer. And each guest went home with a remembrance of the evening: a group photo in our tacky attire.

The party may not have been a "lovely" affair by some standards, but the laughter and camaraderie of our little gathering was genuine.

And that, precious reader, is a memory to cherish. And another reason to LOVE LIFE!

Putting the finishing touches on my column, I marvel at my sense of peace with its contents. Just a few weeks ago, I wouldn't have dared to include such a pedestrian party idea in "The Lovely Life." After all, what would my readers think?

As I hit Send to e-mail my work to the newspaper, I hope my readers are beginning to think of me as a real person who is doing her best with the gifts she's been given — and loving it! (Laundry excluded.)

CHAPTER
TWENTY-SEVEN

LUCY'S BAKED BRIE APPETIZER

1 sheet frozen puff pastry, defrosted
1 small, round Brie cheese
4–5 tablespoons apricot or raspberry preserves
3 tablespoons nuts (walnuts, pecans,
almonds)

Instructions

1. Roll pastry on a lightly floured surface into two circles (a little larger than the round of Brie).
2. Place one circle in a baking pan and center Brie on top of dough.
3. Top Brie with preserves and nuts.
4. Bring the dough up the sides of the cheese and press firmly so it will stay. Top with other circle of dough. Press the two edges of the dough together firmly to seal.

5. Bake in a 375-degree oven for 15–20 minutes or until golden brown.
6. Let stand 10 minutes before transferring to serving dish. Serve with crackers.

Because of our weekend extravaganza, it's been two weeks since we've had FAC, and my hag is beginning to whine. I was excited to see Lucy's e-mail in my inbox, alerting me that she was hosting FAC this week.

As I climb the porch steps to Lucy's front door, I notice two healthy potted mums now grace the entry. Definitely a good sign. I'm even more encouraged when Lucy answers the door.

I no longer expected to see her in the ratty nightgown and rubber-band ponytail, but this time she looks *really* good. A touch of color on her face. Clothes that look like they haven't been pulled from under the bed. And the *pièce dé résistance* — earrings. Let's face it — the last thing a depressed woman is going to think about is putting on earrings.

"Liz! Come in . . . I've missed you," Lucy says cheerfully.

"Me too. Am I the first one here?" I ask, looking around at the tidy but apparently empty home.

"Actually, Kelly and Mary Alice are out back."

"I wondered because I didn't see a car."

"They walked over. Kelly says she's getting a jump on her New Year's resolution to exercise more."

"Come on! It's not even Thanksgiving!"

"Well, you know how goal-oriented Kelly is . . . and this sort of thing is right up M.A.'s alley. She loves being early."

Figures. Just when I've declared the rest of the year a "Back to Carbs Extravaganza."

"Let's go." I head toward the back door. "I don't want to put off my walk through the valley of guilt."

"Before we join the others, I wanted to let you know how much I appreciate all you've done for me these last few weeks."

"Lucy, I didn't — ," I begin.

"Liz, I know you've found yourself out of your comfort zone more times than you care to remember, but you've been there for me. And I'll never forget it."

"Lucy, I've felt bad for not calling you more and —"

She frowns. "Stop it. One thing I'm finally beginning to realize through this process — which is far from over — is to go to the 'throne' before I go to the 'phone.' "

Before I could ask what she meant with all this "throne/phone" business, Jess and Marina arrive at the front door.

"Nothin' says lovin' like somethin' from the oven," sings Marina through the screen door. "What is that great smell?"

"I made Baked Brie Appetizer. It should

be just about done."

"Let me help," Jess offers. "I brought some fruit along. I heard Kelly's going healthy on us again."

Our conversation is relaxed as we sit on Lucy's back deck, enjoying the unusually warm November day. Most likely one of the last.

"It's so peaceful out here," says Mary Alice.

"Not as peaceful as Locust Hill," Lucy replies.

"Won't be able to hear worms chewing on the tomatoes here," I add.

My friends turn to me with puzzled expressions — wondering if my return to carbs is adversely affecting my brain.

I attempt a weak grin. "Never mind. Long story."

"Speaking of long stories," says Lucy, "are you in the mood to hear one? In a way, you all play a part in it."

"I'm always up for stories where I'm the star," Marina jokes.

"I didn't say 'starring' role, but you all have played an important part. This little drama was between me and God."

"We're waiting," says Kelly.

"Well, as you can imagine, the weekend at

Locust Hill gave me a lot to think about. There were many times I wanted to call one — or all — of you to help me process all of it."

"Lucy, you know we would have —," begins Jess.

"That's just it. This time, as I was explaining to Liz earlier, I needed to go to the *throne* before I went to the *phone*."

"Don't I know it, girlfriend," Marina blusters. "There are times when we need to deal directly with the Big Guy."

"Well put, Rina," continues Lucy. "When I came home and looked around at this place, it hit me that I'd been at what my mother used to refer to as a 'pity party' much too long. The only problem was that, other than the dirty dishes, I was getting pretty comfortable at the party. Even starting to enjoy it."

"No!" Kelly covers her ears in mock horror. "Don't tell me you were going to order the Lifetime Movie Network, too!"

"Very funny. To be honest, I realized that if I didn't get a life, Alli would never have the chance to live her own. She'd be too worried about me."

"Either that . . . or she would begin to resent you," Kelly clarifies. "I see it all the time in therapy."

"You're absolutely right, Kelly. I knew I needed to deal with my grief and bitterness," continues Lucy, "but I didn't know where to start."

"I know lots of great therapists," says Kelly.

"I know therapy is great, and I may take you up on your offer later. But as I said, this was one battle that needed to be taken to the *throne.*"

Jess smiles. "I'm so proud of you, Lucy."

"You may take that back when you hear how I went about it."

"I doubt it."

"I felt stuck. Unable to make a decision or sort out my feelings. So I did what Kelly always suggests and put it down on paper."

"Lucy, you know you are creating a monster here," I caution.

"Hey!" says Kelly, fists on her hips.

"Well, it worked. The more I wrote, the more I began to realize that the real problem was that I was angry with God. After all, what had I done to deserve Judd's awful death? And my mom dying? And Alli's going away to school when I was so lonely? The more I railed at God, the more ridiculous I sounded. Even to myself. As if Alli going away to college were some sort of punishment."

423

"Lucy, it's natural to feel — ," Jess starts.

"That's just it," Lucy interrupts. "These may be natural feelings, but the bitterness was hurting not only me but also the person I love the most. Alli. It's not how I want to live."

Lucy takes a deep breath. "So I prayed. Asked for a miracle. I asked God to take away my bitterness, because I knew it was not going to go away on its own."

"So? What happened?" I ask. "You look better than I've seen you in a long time . . . uh, no offense."

Lucy grins. "No offense taken. But to answer your question, not much for a while. Then one day I woke up thinking about Big Henry and the inscription on his gravestone."

"What did it say, Lucy?" asks Mary Alice. "Remember, Kelly and I didn't go out to the cemetery."

"I remember," says Jess. "It said: *The sun never shone so brightly in the heart of a man as it did in the heart of Henry Miller.'*"

"That's it," continues Lucy. "I began to think how wonderful it would be to have such a spirit. And then it dawned on me. Henry had been through much more than I have . . . and probably ever will. He overcame hardship, slavery, discrimination, homelessness, war, illness — and even gave up his dream of moving West so he could help Emily and Anna. If anyone deserved a full blown pity party, it was Big Henry."

"And yet . . . ," I say. Lucy's point is finally beginning to dawn on me.

"That's right, Liz. And yet, *'The sun never shone so brightly in the heart of a man as it did in the heart of Henry Miller.'* Ladies, *I* want to live like Big Henry, and the first step was letting go of my bitterness."

"Lucy, that's so great," says Jess gently.

"Just what I would have advised," teased Kelly.

"I warned you, Luce," I say. "One stray comment . . . and we're going to live with this for years."

"I know what you're thinking, Marina." Lucy looks directly at our uncharacteristically quiet friend.

"I doubt it."

"You're thinking that this is easier said than done. That letting go is a process. That you're not sure you're buying all this."

"That may be some of it."

"I agree. But as you said in Tredway, I come from strong stock. Emily and Joseph Simmons. Anna. Aunt Bette. My mother. And this time I'm not walking alone. I've teamed up with the Big Guy." Lucy winks at Marina.

Marina laughs, breaking the tension. "So what's the next step?"

"Are you ready for this?" Lucy looks around the table, like a little girl who can't wait to tell a secret. "I haven't been so excited about anything for as long as I can remember."

"Come on, Lucy, tell us!" I scoot to the edge of my seat.

"Maybe next FAC . . . just kidding." Lucy laughs. "The idea came to me after looking up the Scripture reference on Emily's grave marker."

"I have to get to that cemetery," Kelly mutters.

"The reference was Micah 6:8. I've already memorized it. It says, *'And what does the LORD require of you but to do justice, to love kindness, and to walk humbly with your God?'* Isn't that beautiful?"

"Yes, but what . . . ?" I ask.

"That's what's so exciting." Lucy's blue eyes are sparkling. "I've decided to continue Emily's work."

Jess looks confused. "I'm not following you, Lucy."

"Me neither," chimes in Kelly.

"What better way to use Locust Hill than to open it up as a shelter for homeless women and their children? I mean, it's a beautiful house in a wonderful setting."

"And with your background in social work, you are just the person to run it," says Jess, clapping her hands in excitement.

"What a great idea!" Kelly declares.

"I agree," I say, "as long as you address the bathroom issue. There's no way more than a couple of women could live there now with just one bathroom."

Lucy nods. "Of course, it will need a lot of work to bring it up to code."

"You know you can count on me — on us," says Mary Alice.

"Maybe Marina can convince Jeff to move up the schedule," Jess suggests. "She seems to have the most sway with him."

Marina swats at the air. "Stop it." Red spots bloom on her cheeks.

"This will be so fun!" I exclaim. "I know several women's groups who might be willing to adopt a room to renovate."

"Just think," says Mary Alice, "an opportunity to design an entire house just for women."

"Maybe a pink bathroom . . . ?" Lucy suggests.

"All the videos will be chick flicks," adds Marina.

"No limit on cookbooks," says Jess.

"And cute sayings on the wall like . . ." Kelly pauses in thought.

I finish my friend's thought. "When life gets sticky, dip it in chocolate!"

"Perfect, Lizzie!" exclaims Lucy as we all explode in laughter.

"Which reminds me," I add, pulling out my bag of chocolate bars, "of another FAC motto: 'Friends don't let friends eat dessert alone.' Dig in, ladies!"

ABOUT THE AUTHOR

Cyndy Salzmann is a wife and mother who does much of her writing on the back of fast-food wrappers — usually while waiting to pick up her kids. Desperate for an excuse to avoid laundry, Cyndy has written three Christian nonfiction books on home management for the domestically challenged, launched a national speaking career, worked as a Christian radio personality, and taught her children how to sort colors. *Dying to Decorate* is her first novel and the first title in the Friday Afternoon Club mystery series.

Cyndy has been married for twenty-four years to John Salzmann, her college sweetheart and the most patient man in the world. They are blessed with three children: Freddy (19), Liz (17), and Anna (13). And, yes, the family also has a precocious Westie named Daisy, who loves to scavenge in the trash.

In her spare time, Cyndy loves to cook, read, and work on family scrapbooks. This last pursuit allows her to permanently destroy any photos of herself she doesn't consider flattering.

Finally, but most importantly, Cyndy loves God with all her heart and has committed her life to following His lead, even if it means airing all her dirty laundry. Literally.

Nonfiction Titles by Cyndy Salzmann
Making Your Home a Haven: Strategies for the Domestically Challenged
The Occasional Cook: Culinary Strategies for Overcommitted Families
Beyond Groundhogs and Gobblers: Putting Meaning into Your Holiday Celebrations

Want to Contact Cyndy?
You may write her via e-mail at cyndy@familyhavenministries.com, through her Web site: www.familyhavenministries.com, or to:

Family Haven Ministries
15905 Jones Cr.
Omaha, NE 68118

A free subscription to her newsletter is

available by sending a blank e-mail to subscribe@familyhavenministries.com.

The employees of Thorndike Press hope you have enjoyed this Large Print book. All our Thorndike and Wheeler Large Print titles are designed for easy reading, and all our books are made to last. Other Thorndike Press Large Print books are available at your library, through selected bookstores, or directly from us.

For information about titles, please call:
(800) 223-1244

or visit our Web site at:
http://gale.cengage.com/thorndike

To share your comments, please write:
Publisher
Thorndike Press
295 Kennedy Memorial Drive
Waterville, ME 04901